```
F                          06-2106
McK      McKeever, Kate                  ✓
              The single file
```

	DATE DUE		
MY 09 07			
MY 30 07			
JE 27 07			
JY 18 07			
OCT 0 3 2007			
NOV 0 7 2007			
DEC 1 5 2010			
AUG 1 0 2011			
SEP 2 6 2012			

Somersworth Public Library
25 Main Street
Somersworth, NH 03878

THE SINGLE FILE

Other books by Kate McKeever:

The Single Life

THE SINGLE FILE

•

Kate McKeever

AVALON BOOKS
NEW YORK

© Copyright 2007 by S. Griffith
All rights reserved.
All the characters in the book are fictitious,
and any resemblance to actual persons,
living or dead, is purely coincidental.
Published by Thomas Bouregy & Co., Inc.
160 Madison Avenue, New York, NY 10016

Library of Congress Cataloging-in-Publication Data

McKeever, Kate, 1957–
    The single file / Kate McKeever.
      p. cm.
    ISBN 978-0-8034-9822-8 (acid-free paper)
    1. Women journalists—Fiction. 2. Atlanta (Ga.)—Fiction.
I. Title.

PS3613.C5526S55 2007
813'.6—dc22

                                                 2006101340

PRINTED IN THE UNITED STATES OF AMERICA
ON ACID-FREE PAPER
BY HADDON CRAFTSMEN, BLOOMSBURG, PENNSYLVANIA

To my father, for instilling the desire to learn, and to my mother, for giving me the determination to follow my dreams. Thank you, and I love you.

My thanks to the ladies and gent of SMRW, you're the best! And thanks to my critique group, Kerri, Katie, Juli, Sue and Erin, and Donna; your task is monumental at times, keeping me on the straight and narrow.

Chapter One

"If you ask me, the worst thing you could do for that column is give it to the ice queen."

Caroline Paul grimaced as she passed the business editor's desk. Just because she'd declined his offers for a second date, time and time again, it wasn't a good enough reason to deny her a shot at the *Single Life* column. Thank goodness he didn't have the final say.

When her friend, Laney, had recommended her for the spot in writing the popular column, Caroline had taken it as a lark. Covering the singles' events in the Atlanta area proved enjoyable and kept her busy, even if it, along with her society column, were looked upon as fluff. And after all, she didn't need the column for career advancement. As society reporter, she was in a spot that ensured she could make a living—if not an extravagant one—at the newspaper game. So she didn't possess the competitive nature Laney had, or want to advance to more "meaty" stories. At least she was happy in her job without the ambition.

Caroline dropped her purse into the drawer of her desk and took her seat. After a few minutes of perusing her notes she completed the society column piece on the charity fashion show, then focused on the latest installment of *The Single Life.*

The column originated when the city editor forced Laney and Grant, two of *Atlanta Globe's* reporters, into a weekly column. Laney, notorious for being a loner and avoiding relationships, had to go online, logon to a matchmaker website, place personal ads, and then follow through with dates, all shadowed by Grant. The two, "serious" journalists battled both the perceived embarrassment of the column and their attraction to each other. Now, after a year, they were happily dating and supervised *The Single Life* columns, now syndicated in five newspapers in the southeast.

Caroline actually had fun with the column and all the dating opportunities it presented. So far, she'd had dates two or three nights a week and, if they all didn't turn out well, she still had the chance to meet "Mr. Maybe."

She scanned a few of the online ads she'd received in the past week. She began the preparation for her article only to be interrupted by a phone call.

"Hello." Caroline tucked the receiver between her ear and shoulder and tapped at her computer keyboard.

"Hey, kiddo. Got any news for us?" The deep tones of Grant Stone rumbled across the line.

Caroline grinned. "Yep. I'm in love."

"What?"

She giggled at the shock in Grant's tone. "Well, it worked for you, why not me?"

"It didn't work in a month, though. What's going on, for real?" Grant wondered.

"For real, I've had a total of fifteen dates in the past month and I've yet to meet a guy that I'd date more than once."

"Now that sounds familiar." Laney's voice chirped over the line.

"Listening in again, sugar?" Caroline recognized her twinge of envy at the purr in Grant's voice. He might act like a hard nosed reporter around everyone else, but he melted at the sight of Delaney Morgan.

Caro grinned at the banter that ensued when Laney lit into Grant for calling her an endearment. He loved needling her friend and Caro suspected Laney enjoyed sparring with him as much.

She envied the pair their ease with each other,

their openness. After years of being coworkers, they'd progressed to love in the space of months.

Her experiences with men, while a bit different than Laney, resulted in the same result no matter whom she dated. She'd been burned too many times.

"The Ice Princess" had reason to be cool around men. She possessed the beauty of a modern Grace Kelly, had always been "the pretty one." Early on, though, she quit relying on her beauty and instead depended on brains. Indeed, the fact that she could have strode down a model's runway proved to be as much of a detriment as an asset.

"Caro?" Laney's interruption of her thoughts was welcome.

"Hey, still here." She absently thumbed through the paper copies of matches she'd had in the past week in the on-line matching service. Not a one jumped out at her, even though several of them were reasonably attractive, one even gorgeous.

"Honey, are you okay?" Laney sounded concerned. She knew Caro too well.

"Yeah, I'm fine. Just looking over the next several prospects."

"Any octogenarians?" Grant chimed in.

"Ha, ha."

"She doesn't have a partner who's trying to sabotage her like I did, sweetheart." Laney reminded him of his machinations during their time with the column.

"And good thing I did. You would have gotten away, otherwise." His voice deepened.

"I think I'm too young to listen to this." Caro grinned.

"Have you found anyone that looks promising, hon?"

"Several look that way at the beginning, Laney. The problem is meeting them again after the first date." She propped her hand on her chin and tossed the pile of papers aside.

"Are you still okay with doing the column? It's not the most comfortable situation to be in—being a dating guinea pig for the public."

Caro sighed. "Tell me about it. I promised you I'd give the column six months and it's only been four. I'm willing to stick it out for the rest of the time." Caro paused as a thought occurred to her. "Unless the ratings are down. If that's the case—"

"No, ratings are as good as ever. The readers love hearing about the foibles of the modern single woman. All of the syndicated cities' numbers are healthy, including Atlanta." Grant's calm tone assured Caro she still had her job, as a dating klutz at least.

Caro decided to change the subject, seeing how

depressing the whole topic was. "So, how is Tampa? Sunny and gorgeous?"

"Hot and humid. It's April and it's eighty-nine degrees, for cripes' sake." Laney responded.

"Take advantage of the weather and go to the beach. I'm still wearing my sweater." Caro grinned. She couldn't imagine Laney lying on the beach. Rather her best friend would be competing in sand castle contests, daring a fisherman to show her how to catch a sailfish, or worse. The idea of Laney, or Grant for that matter, staying in one spot for any period of time was unheard of.

"We'll be back home this evening." Grant inserted. "And not a minute too soon. Laney wants to check on the Braves' status."

"Like they can't get along without you?" Caro chuckled.

"Nope, can't. Listen, kiddo, I'll call you when I get in and we'll shoot on over to BR, okay?" Laney urged.

"Sure thing. I've not had rocky road in over a month."

The two women spent a lot of time commiserating at Baskin Robbins over calorie-laden ice cream when one had to talk things over. That Laney picked up on her discontent was just an indication of their friendship. And their joint track record in dating before Laney got lucky with Grant.

Caro's Palm Pilot beeped and she glanced toward the clock. Three thirty. "Laney, I've got to go. I've got a tea function to cover in Buckhead."

"Keep at it, kiddo. We'll see you when we get back." Caro ended the conversation with a promise to meet the couple for lunch after they came back to town.

She grabbed her purse and headed to the parking lot. Another society luncheon, given by a Buckhead housewife, another plate of warm cucumber sandwiches, lukewarm tea, and soggy cake. Yep, such is the life of a society column reporter.

The event had the requisite faces to photograph, quotes to take, and names to drop. While Caro might have a column, a coup in the world of journalism, she also was the photographer. After assurances she would have the proofs for the hostess to check in a few days, she headed back to the office.

As she drove down the country lane off the main highway, Caro let her thoughts wander to the online ads she'd received over the past couple of days. She really should give the phone executive a chance. He was cute, gainfully employed, and willing to meet early on in the communication. After talking to Laney and Grant, she became more aware of the fact she was alone—truly alone.

The car sputtered a couple of times, alarming her. She slowed down, and then after a particularly scary sputter the engine stopped. She managed to get the car off the road and pulled to the shoulder.

"Great, just great." She crawled from the car, although why she didn't know. The extent of her knowledge of car repair was to clean the ashtray of credit card receipts and quarters before taking it to the auto detailer.

She strode to the front of the car, kicking up orange dust. After several moments' struggle she managed to find the latch that popped the hood to the ancient Volvo sedan and lifted the heavy metal covering. Nothing steamed, no leaks that she could see. Nothing at all.

A survey of the road around her revealed no cars approaching. No knights in shining armor today. She closed the hood and then leaned into the car to retrieve her cell phone when her eyes lit on the gas gauge.

"I didn't get gas before I left," she groaned and dropped her head in defeat. The conversation with Laney had distracted her enough that her normal routine of checking for supplies, including sufficient fuel for the trips she had to take, had escaped her.

Now, she was stranded on a two lane road, one oddly empty for this area of Georgia, with no gas and no visible help.

"And in high heels, yet." She glanced at her fashionable shoes. They'd been perfect for the tea she'd covered for the paper. Still, the two-inch heels would be murder on any walk.

She opened the cell phone and dialed. Nothing. Caro pulled the phone away from her ear and glared at the tiny screen. No signal. No signal, no gas, no choice.

Since there hadn't been anything in the way of a gas station on her way from the tea, she continued down the road toward the main highway and Atlanta proper.

After several minutes of walking she growled in frustration. Nothing, except her aching feet, trees, and dust. Up ahead a lone road broke off to the right. Seeing that as her only option, Caro trudged on and broke off the main road.

Farther down the smaller road an old fashioned building squatted, ancient gas tanks stationed outside. "Hope they had a gallon or two in them," she muttered. The garage bay was open and someone stirred inside.

As she approached, Caro heard voices and laughter, along with the sounds of metal banging against metal.

"Hello?" She hobbled to the gas pumps and leaned against one, fighting the urge to take off a heel and rub her feet.

"Be right with you." The voice came from deep within the garage.

Caro made her way to the entrance of the bay and peered inside. No one, no owner of the disembodied voice. A car resided in the main area that she recognized as a classic from her dealings with the rich and infamous.

"I've run out of gas—"

"Hold on. Coming up."

A hand appeared around the edge of the underside of the car and he appeared from a deep well, hoisting himself out of the work area under the car.

Every preconceived notion she'd ever had about mechanics flew from Caro's head as she surveyed the man approaching her. He wore a tight gray t-shirt and jeans, both slightly stained with dirt. He wiped his hands on a rag and eyed her in return.

"You ran out of gas, you say?" A voice from behind her startled Caro and she spun around. A man in a wheelchair rolled toward her, his long shoulder-length brown hair flowing around his shoulders.

"Yes," She smiled at him, and getting a disarming grin in return.

"Gus, we need to help this lady out." He came to a stop beside Caro.

"Just getting to it, Trav. Where's your car?" The hunk approached her and Caro returned her attention to him. His brown hair was highlighted with some lighter streaks, almost blond and his topaz eyes studied her steadily. His face, rugged with sharply honed angles wasn't classically handsome but she was drawn to him all the same.

"I left it out on the main road, maybe half a mile away."

"And walked in those shoes?" Trav glanced down at her heels drawing her attention back to him. Caro was used to men admiring her, it wasn't new. She shrugged her shoulders slightly.

"I couldn't get a signal on my cell so I didn't have a lot of choice."

"We have that problem around here sometimes, especially when the weather is iffy, like today." Trav chattered on about the April weather in Georgia and the clouds that scuttled across the sky in the late afternoon. Caro listened with half an ear as she followed Gus's movements.

He silently retrieved a gas can and passed her and her talkative companion. Caro watched as he urged fuel from the old, oddly shaped gas pumps. Finally, he acknowledged her presence and turned to her.

"What make of car do you have?"

"A Volvo 760. It's the only one that was pulled over on the side of the road when I left." She replied archly, a little put out that he wasn't more friendly. She wasn't used to men being rude to her, at least until she'd rebuffed them.

"Don't want to put gas in the wrong car, just in case. Be right back." He strode toward a pickup truck parked nearby.

"You aren't going without me." She scampered off after him, all the while wondering why she would accompany him instead of sitting with the more amiable Trav.

"Suit yourself." He unlocked and opened the passenger side door for her. Caro had to hike up her straight skirt to maneuver into the truck, but she did so without help and without embarrassing herself, but barely.

She watched through the passenger rear view mirror as he deposited the gas can in the bed of the truck and walked around to his door. Again, in silence he entered the truck and started the engine.

"Thanks for helping." She decided to be civil.

"No problem."

"I normally don't make a practice of running out of gas, but—" Why was she explaining herself? Obviously he didn't care one way or another whether she planned ahead or not.

"Happens to us all every now and then." He glanced at her and she felt him taking in her outfit. The spring suit, conservative and classic, screamed money. What was he thinking? Whatever it was, Caro was sure it wouldn't be accurate. Or complimentary, from his stern expression.

"Which way?" He came to a stop at the end of the lane.

"To the left." She leaned forward. Yep, there it was. Her trusty, ugly square car.

He pulled beyond her car and exited. Caro followed him and watched as he opened the gas cap and filled her car. All too soon, he straightened and turned to her. "Try to start it. It may need priming."

Whatever that meant. She unlocked the door and perched on the driver's seat, her legs remaining out of the car. She twisted the key and after a couple of sputters the engine started. She turned with a ready smile, determined to be nice.

He leaned against the car, his eyes on her legs. Well, he was more aware of her than he'd let on, she grinned a little, really glad for once of her looks and genetics.

Gus eyed the woman in front of him. Slim, cool and almost too beautiful, she didn't fit the Georgia countryside around them. In fact, she didn't look as if she belonged outside of movie films. Her slim features and classic style looked more in keeping with a forties starlet.

And the legs on her. He'd kept his distance as he refilled her gas tank, all the time aware of her behind him, her light perfume teasing his senses.

"How much do I owe you?" She smiled up at him, drawing his attention away from her feet in those heels.

"Nothing."

"Oh, come on. I pulled you away from your work and caused you to leave your friend—"

"Actually, Travis owns the garage with me."

"Sorry. Anyway, I need to pay you something for your trouble." Her smile, flirtation in its purest form, tugged at him.

"No problem. Have a good day, and remember to get gas this time." He ignored the urge to talk to her more, to check out her ring finger, and headed back to his truck. A hard twist of the key and he was on his way.

He arrived at the garage to find Travis at the work bench, the carburetor from the classic Grand Am in front of him. Gus bypassed the bay and entered the tiny office in the front of the building. The coffee urn was empty so he refilled the carafe with water and loaded the coffee maker with fresh grounds. A few minutes later he joined Travis in the bay with two cups filled with the brew.

"Did you get her squared away?" Travis leaned away from his work rebuilding the carburetor and accepted the coffee.

"Yeah, she's gone."

"Too bad. She was pretty easy on the eye."

Gus grunted as he sipped his coffee. His friend eyed him steadily.

"She was interested, you know."

"No, thanks." Gus reached around his friend and shifted the carburetor to examine it.

"What do you mean? Man, that woman was fine. Nice figure, friendly, and a face that'd stop traffic."

"Not interested."

"Ha. That's a flat out lie and you know it. I saw the gleam in your eye, friend. And I've known you too long to believe it's axle grease."

Gus met Travis' gaze. "And you know my record. I've had one too many dealings with women that are more interested in fashion and what money can buy than in building a lasting relationship."

"She didn't seem—"

"No, Trav. Not again." The last woman he'd been interested in, serious about, had decided she liked his bank account more than she loved him. The fact that it took three years before he found it out, as well as an aborted trip to the altar, still stung. He'd been burned one too many times. No. No more society girls for him.

Caro steamed for a while as she drove home. Even as he helped her, Gus the Grudging One had also left her with the impression she had a large kick me sign on her back.

"What was the matter with me that he couldn't even make nice?" She muttered over the road noise that crept through her car's inadequate insulation.

It had been years since she'd gotten that kind of

reception. Usually men reacted more like Travis, eager to help, friendly. Instead, Gus had treated her with cool politeness, the same as he'd treat any customer, she'd bet.

"And I stood there and took it."

Well, it'd be different next time. If there was a next time.

Chapter Two

"You mean he didn't ask you out?" Laney scooped a spoonful of pralines and cream into her mouth.

"No. He just refused my offer to pay for the gas and left." Caro stirred the mush that used to be Chocolate Mint and sighed. Her first instinct upon returning to her house had been to call Laney with an emergency Baskin Robbins call. Laney's appearance at Caro's apartment, ice cream in tow, eased a bit of her tension. At least she had her friend to offer condolences.

"Well, that's a first."

"What's that supposed to mean?" She looked away from the melting mass and toward Laney.

"Just that you get more invites for dates in a week

than I did in the entire time I did the *Single Life* column. Let's face it, Caro. You're gorgeous."

"Lot of good it does me," Caro groused and gave up on the ice cream. She stood up from her easy chair and strode toward the kitchen. "Want a glass of iced tea?"

"With pralines and cream? Eww." Laney shook her head.

"We could combine it with the ice cream, sort of like sodas or floats. Sugar and caffeine, all you could want in a drink." Caro tried for a joke but didn't put any feeling behind it. She poured a glass of tea for herself and some ice water for Laney. She carried the drinks to the living room and plopped back down into her ancient easy chair.

Laney accepted her water and set it on the coffee table in front of the sofa she lounged on. "Why are you so bent out of shape about this Gus guy, anyway? It's not like you're interested—"

Caro feigned attention on her drink and the craft show playing on her television.

"You *are* interested in him?" Laney sat up and pushed her own bowl away.

"Of course not. I was thinking of using it in the column. You know, how you meet people and—"

"And you haven't been upset whether a man paid attention to you or not in the past. Is he cute?" Laney grinned.

"Yes," Caro sighed.

"Tell me."

"He's got brown hair, streaked with blond, naturally I think. And these cat eyes. Topaz."

"And the body?"

"Nice." Caro shrugged.

Laney snorted. "Nice. If it was just nice, you wouldn't be thinking about him right now. Now, give."

"All right. He's not that handsome. The guy he works with is better looking, but there's something about him, you know?"

Laney's grin dimmed but the understanding in her eyes scared Caro more than the teasing irritated her. "I know exactly what you're saying."

"It's not what you think. He just got on my nerves by being so rude."

"I thought you said he was polite."

"But he was rude when he was polite." Caro grimaced at her friend. "Never mind. I don't want to talk about it any more."

Laney smiled gently then changed the subject. "Okay, let's talk about the column."

"Yippee."

"I thought you were having fun with it."

Caro waved a hand dismissively and raised her glass. "I am. Sorry, just in a rotten mood. Go on." She sipped her iced tea, searching for calm.

"Grant and I were talking the other day. We need

to come up with something different for you. You're doing fine," Laney consoled Caro, "but we want something a little different."

"I'm not doing an auction or anything like that."

Laney chuckled. "Grant'd love it, but no. I wouldn't do anything to you that I wouldn't do myself. I was thinking along the lines of specialized group outings."

"Come again?" She might need another serving of ice cream for this.

"In the other cities we oversee, there are specialized single groups. Jewish singles, single athletes, and singles who do charity work. That sort of thing."

Caro perked up a bit. "I see. So you want me to find the specialized groups and highlight them?"

Laney nodded. "It might give the readership a better idea of the diversified singles in the area. I felt like a lot of people out there thought that only people who were willing to go online and answer newspaper ads were somehow marginalized. I want to let them know there's room for everyone in the singles' scene."

"It'd give a different slant on it, that's for sure." And it'd give her a chance to branch out a bit, get away from the first impression she made on men when they saw her picture in online ads.

"Great. I'll let Grant and Mr. Phipps know you're on board with the idea." Laney leaned back and propped her feet on the coffee table. She looked eager to return to the subject of Gus so Caro turned the topic to Laney and Grant's travels supervising the *Single Life* columns.

All the next day Caro divided her time between writing up the previous day's society tea and researching special interest singles' groups in the greater Atlanta area. The entire time, though, a face swam in front of her—a rugged striking face with clear, intense eyes, judging her. By the end of the day she'd almost convinced herself she didn't care whether he liked her or not, whether he thought her attractive or not.

She leafed through the photos of the tea guests and hostess. Something was missing. The exterior shot of the house was off center and a bit blurry. It'd have to be done again.

Instead of e-mailing it to the editor, as usual, she printed the article out and strode to Ms. English's office. The office door, closed as usual, couldn't quite muffle the rumble of drums from within. Caro took a bracing breath then pounded on the door.

"Enter!"

She cracked the door open an inch, ready for the blast of heavy metal; still she felt the percussion. As she entered Caro yelled, "I wanted to ask you for an opinion."

"What?" The attractive middle-aged woman looked away from her computer monitor.

"I said—" Caro inched a couple of feet farther.

"Hold on a minute." Julia English spun her chair and with a flick of her hand silenced the repetitive beat of drums and wail of electric guitars. As she closed the office door behind her Caro acknowledged a distant 'thank you' from the newsroom with a grin.

"What'd you need?" Julia reached for a packet of no smoking gum. Remains of gum wrappers cluttered her desk, testifying to the struggle the editor was having to break a long-standing habit. She ripped the paper from the small wafer of gum and stuffed it in her mouth then waved her hand toward Caro in a gesture to proceed.

Caro fidgeted before approaching the editor's desk then handed the tea column to Ms. English and plunged in, "I think there's something missing in this piece."

"And you're asking *me* about a society column?"

Good point. The woman had cut her teeth on gritty crime stories. Caro wondered how she managed to oversee the features columns, or even wanted the job.

"I just need a day's extension; I need to get a couple more photos."

"Well, I guess the world will have to live without knowing what the rich and idle are doing for fun."

"Right." Caro drawled, quelling the urge to roll her eyes at the editor's sarcasm.

"Whatever. I'll find some filler for tomorrow's edition. Just be happy you don't want an extension on the single's column. You wouldn't stand a chance with Wheaton."

Julia waved Caro out of the office and immediately after she shut the door music surged through the walls.

Caro grabbed her purse and camera bag and sprinted as fast as her leather flats could carry her toward the exit of the newsroom.

"Caroline."

She halted just inside the exit and slowly turned to face Franklin Jones. Not Frank, not Jonesy. Franklin.

"What can I do for you, Franklin? I'm on my way out."

"Go to a concert with me tomorrow night." His voice grated on her nerves.

"No thanks."

His thin face flushed. "You didn't even ask what concert."

She breathed in a sigh and kept her patience. "I'm sure it'll be a nice concert, but I can't go. I'm on assignment." *Or I will be when I find somewhere to go.*

"Right." Franklin shifted his weight before continuing, "Why haven't you agreed to go out with me again? We had fun on the outing to the Junior League benefit."

"No reason. I've just been busy." She edged toward the exit, eager to escape his pestering.

"You don't want to go out with me anymore, do you?"

Caro sighed. She'd wanted to avoid a scene, especially at the newspaper. And even if she didn't have the ambition Laney had, she still knew it'd seal her reputation in stone if she told Franklin exactly what she thought of him. Instead, she sent him the practiced smile that worked with all men.

"Let's compromise. Since I can't attend the concert, why don't we go to lunch or dinner the day after?"

"Dinner." He gloated and Caro realized she'd just been maneuvered.

"Fine, dinner it is. I'll talk to you more about it tomorrow, okay?"

She managed to get away a few minutes later, her temper intact but pride a bit bruised. Why didn't he take her refusals at face value?

She made her way to the exclusive neighborhood in Buckhead and made short work of taking enough exterior shots of the tea location to fill a magazine spread. On the way back, down the infamous country road, she finally admitted to herself, she wanted to stop and try again with Gus.

"He'll just make Franklin look more appealing." She muttered as she made the turn onto the lane and headed toward the cinderblock garage.

The bay was open to the spring air, as it had been

the day before, but little noise came from its depths. Caro parked the car out of the way of the gas pumps and approached the garage bay.

"Hello? Anyone home?"

"Come on in, in the back." The voice, pleasant though it was, had a higher timber than Gus's. Caro followed the sound and rounded the corner of the classic car parked in the center of the one car bay.

At a low worktable sat Trav, Gus's friend and business partner. His hands were greasy and dirty and in front of him lay a metal hunk, presumably a car part.

"Sorry, am I interrupting something?" Caro smiled.

"Nah. I'm just rebuilding this carburetor. A dirty business and as boring as it gets." He pushed away from the table and advanced toward Caro. "Is your car okay?"

She saw him glance over her shoulder and hastened to reassure him. "Yes, it's fine. I just wanted to stop by and thank you and Gus again for your help. I'm Caroline Paul, by the way."

"Travis McIntyre. Want something to drink? I'm going to get myself a soda." He rolled toward a door, pausing at a sink to quickly scrub his hands. Caro followed him slowly.

"Thanks, if you have a diet, that'd be great."

Was Gus here? She didn't hear any other sounds. Maybe he was off rescuing and insulting another stranded driver. "Gus wouldn't let me pay for the gas or his time yesterday."

Travis opened the door to an old fashioned chest style soda machine and extracted two bottles of soda. He handed Caro one and twisted open the cap of his drink. After taking a long draught, he grinned at her.

"Well, of course he wouldn't. It's not done. You're a pretty girl and he's a man. It would have been an insult to you if he had taken the money."

"So it was a compliment that he was short and rude and—"

"A jerk?" Travis laughed. "Pretty much. Gus isn't known for his manners or easy way of talking."

But his friend was. He could charm the birds out of the trees, if he wanted.

"Well, he must have really liked me, cause he couldn't wait to get out of my sight." Caro glanced around before continuing, "Do I need to worry about getting complimented again?"

"Nope. He's out on other business today. Just me and the boys." Travis indicated others' presence with a tilt of his head. Caro bent her own head and sipped her soda from the bottle to hide the disappointment in her eyes. She could hide it from Travis but not from herself.

"Well, I won't keep you from your work." She set

the soda on the glass counter and shouldered her purse again, intent on leaving.

"What's your hurry? You haven't met the boys." Travis didn't give her time to make excuses but leaned back and yelled over his shoulder. "Haggis! Buford! Come meet our company."

After a few seconds' silence, Caro heard the click of-heels? No, not heels. A couple of overweight, droopy eyed basset hounds appeared at the doorway, their tails wagging in perfect time to each other.

"Caroline, meet the boys. Boys, be nice, she's quality." Travis sent a stern eye at the pair and Caro wondered what they could do, stare at her until she broke down in tears? The multicolored basset approached first, his eyes shining and his stubby legs pounding at the floor. Caro bent to him and petted his head, gently scratching behind his ears. "Hey, boy. Pleased to meet you—" and she looked curiously at Travis.

"That's Buford. The more outgoing one. Haggis'll come around though. He's shy."

Caro bit off a chuckle at the sight in front of her. Haggis, a brown and white dog, stood a few feet off, his tail wagging his whole back end. As she scratched Buford's ears, she murmured to both dogs. Suddenly Haggis moved quicker than she'd expect and plopped in front of her, his head cocked toward her, ears first. She laughed and obligingly scratched.

"They're beautiful."

Travis grinned wider, "That's the first time I've heard them described that way. Gus originally meant to get a guard dog, seeing as how we have some pretty expensive collector cars in the bay at times. When he showed up with these guys, I knew he'd been had."

"Did he get them at a pet store?"

"No, at the animal shelter. Their owner lived in an apartment and these boys howled whenever she'd leave til she got threatened with either eviction or getting rid of the dogs."

"I think Gus got the better deal." Caro gently patted the dogs' heads one last time. Sensing she was finished with them, the animals retreated and settled at the foot of Travis's wheelchair.

"We both did. What they don't have in meanness, they make up for in barking. Sound like they're going to eat you up."

"Thanks for introducing me but I really do have to go now. I have some photos to develop." Caro retrieved the purse she'd dropped when greeting the dogs and made for the exterior door. Travis followed her and halted just outside the building.

"You a photographer?"

"No, I work at the *Atlanta Globe*. I'm a reporter."

"Well, don't make yourself scarce. I'll tell Gus you stopped by."

Caro took a few steps towards her car, suddenly very unsure of herself and any reference to Gus.

"That's okay. I was just in the area and wanted to thank you. Thanks for the soda."

"No problem, it was a nice break for me." Travis waved her off, his expression pleasant.

Now, why couldn't she be attracted to him, rather than his moody friend?

"She's a reporter."

"Who?" Gus kept his head buried deep in the engine of the Dodge, his attention on loosening a bolt.

"The looker who ran out of gas the other day. She came by yesterday. Name's Caroline Paul."

"So? You didn't take any money from her, did you?" Gus lifted his head enough to glare at Travis.

"You know better than that. She stayed awhile, met the boys and left. After she asked about you, that is."

Gus dove back into the depths of the engine. Nothing was worse for him than the cool beauty of the lady he couldn't get his mind off of.

A few minutes of silence followed, save the comforting sounds he associated with the garage, metal clanging against metal, the tinny sound of the small radio churning out country songs, and the shuffle of the dogs as they sought water, a soft spot or something to investigate in the bay.

"Don't tell me you aren't going to do something about it."

Gus heaved a sigh and pulled himself out of the depths of the car.

"You're as bad as Haggis with a bone, man."

Travis tossed down the rag he'd been cleaning the carburetor with and swiveled his chair to face Gus.

"Maybe I'm not willing to see you make an ass of yourself again."

"Then leave off on Caroline." He glared at his friend.

"She's different, and you know it, Gus."

Gus stalked to the tool chest and tossed his wrench on top of the bench surface. "Damn it. You haven't seen her more than two times, talked to her, what, around half an hour? And you know her personality, her values. Give me a break."

"I'm saying she doesn't know who you are. She thinks you own a garage. In her eyes you're just the man who pulled her out of a jam. Evidently—a man she's attracted to, or she wouldn't have shown up here."

Gus stared at his friend. Travis had been there when Alicia snowed him into thinking she'd fallen in love with him, the man, not the money and position.

Caroline possessed the same beauty. Gus recognized the designer clothing, the shoes that cost more than the average person made in a month. He'd bet a mint the older car she drove was the aberration, a trophy from a breakup or a treasured heirloom. Not a necessity.

"I just don't want the aggravation, Trav. Not anymore."

Travis reached for his rag and cleaning solution. "Well, just remember to lube every now and then, cause without exercise that ticker of yours is going to rust. Fast."

Chapter Three

"What do you think of the restaurant?" Franklin smiled broadly, his eyes in constant motion. From her to the crowd milling around, back to her and then to her chest.

Caro forced a smile toward the man, all the while gritting her teeth. It was her worst nightmare all over again. "I like it just fine, Franklin."

"I had to call in a few favors for the table, but once the maitré d understood who I was, he caved."

God, let this be over soon.

"I'm sure he was very accommodating." Caro accepted the drink the waiter set in front of her and took a grateful sip of her tonic.

Franklin snorted. "Hardly. But when you're a

business editor, you learn to pull your weight. Especially with lesser beings."

Caro quit biting her tongue at that. Too many of her friends spent long years as waiters and bartenders, earning college money.

"I don't agree."

"Really? You've never used your position as a tool?"

"Not if I can avoid it. But that's not what I'm talking about. I don't agree with your attitudes toward other people."

"I don't have an attitude." Franklin actually bristled.

"I think you do. When you call someone a lesser being, especially someone who spends eight to ten hours on their feet, trying to appease snobby people who think they're entitled to more privilege just because they wear a suit to work or have a degree or—"

"You're criticizing me?"

"You bet I am." Caro leaned forward to press her point. "I used to be one of the lesser life forms and I had to deal with mauling and innuendoes and more for too many years."

Franklin threw down the napkin he'd been dabbing his forehead with. "I shouldn't have to put up with this. Not from a society reporter," he sneered. "Nobody is that good looking."

"You're right, you shouldn't have to put up with it. And I'm not going to make you endure another minute of my company."

As she picked up her light jacket and purse and strode from the restaurant into the night, Caro's spirits lifted. *At last, I'm having an enjoyable minute in the evening.*

Caro smiled in relief as she replaced the phone receiver the next day. After three hours of internet research, she'd found several specialty singles' groups. A quick elimination of the inappropriate, the hunting clubs and those with one member, she came up with fifteen groups. She then chose the groups with imminent meetings, Sporty Singles, Singles for Charity, and an unnamed group that met weekly for board games.

She called and got directions for the meetings. The first was that weekend and the last two were the following week. As she jotted the meetings in her calendar, Caro glanced at the last week's appointments.

The afternoon tea, followed by three fashion shows, and a dinner and dance. "God, my life is pathetic," she groaned.

"Right. And I have the golden life." Laney dropped into the chair beside Caro's desk.

"Don't give me that. You've got a great guy who

understands you, who loves you, and you're happy in your job—"

"Since when aren't you happy? And I didn't say I was unhappy. I'm just tired from traveling to Charlotte and back in three days."

Caro flicked off the power to the computer monitor, shutting off the images of tropical fish swimming lazily across the screen. "Sorry. I just realized something."

"What?" Laney fiddled with Caro's desk calendar, her eyes steady on her friend.

"That my life is spent as an outsider." Caro glanced around the suddenly stifling newsroom. "I need to get out of here. Want to go get something to drink?"

"Sure. Let's go to the coffee shop—"

"No, I need something a little stronger."

Laney grinned, "Another BR run?"

"Yep. This conversation calls for a chocolate malt."

The pair chose Caro's car to make the trip to Baskin Robbins and on the way chatted about Laney's trip to Charlotte and other mundane things. After Caro received her malted milkshake and Laney her double scoop, they retreated to a small table in the rear of the almost deserted restaurant.

"So give," Laney scooped a healthy spoonful of ice cream.

"I had an epiphany."

"Ouch, I hate those."

Caro snorted. "It wasn't a hangnail."

"Just as painful and not nearly as easy to deal with." Laney gestured with her spoon, "Go on. What brought on this clarity of thought?"

"I just realized that I spend the better part of my life watching other people live their lives. And then writing about it."

"That's called being a reporter, kid. It's what we do."

"Not all of us. Some of us have a relationship. Look at you." Caro pointed a finger at Laney. "You and Grant decided to work on your relationship and you're still together, even after months."

"And the operative word is work."

Caro didn't sense any tension in Laney's voice, but then she'd been focused on herself. "Are you guys doing okay?"

Laney grinned, a slight flush creeping across her cheeks. "Really well. I'm just agreeing with you, we have to work on the relationship. But the nicest part of this is that I *want* to work on it."

"See? That's my point. I don't have that. I don't have anything of substance in my life." Caro glanced down at her outfit. A shell pink pencil skirt, paired with a white sweater set and the recently back-in-fashion pink pearls. "Look at me. I'm all surface and no essence."

"Now you've lost me." Laney glanced at her outfit in confusion.

"I wear the costumes I need to get into the afternoon teas and garden parties, or dinner dances. I don't have a style or anything to call my own. I only have the outsider's perspective, the observer's costume."

Laney shoved the ice cream cup away, her attention diverted. "This is serious."

"Yeah, I guess it is."

"Honey, you've got more substance than you know. The clothes? The hair, all of it—" Laney gestured toward Caro. "It's not you, just like the clothes I wear aren't me, or the godawful Braves jacket Grant has from his college days isn't really him."

"But they *do* reflect personality."

"They reflect style. And you have it to spare."

"Yeah, style." Caro kept seeing Gus's face in her mind. He didn't care about her clothes or shoes. Was he the reason she had so much trouble with this?

"Some people have it, naturally. When we were in college you managed to look good in the sweats we wore to run. Even sweaty, you look good."

"That's not something I can take to the bank, Laney."

"Actually you could have, and you know it."

"Well, I can't take it to the altar or relationship couch."

Laney suddenly stood and, scooping up the ice cream remains, marched to the trash. After depositing the containers in the can, she wheeled around. "Come on."

"I'm not ready to go back to the office."

"We're not. We're going for a ride."

"Okay." Caro followed her friend out of the building and handed over the keys.

Laney drove in silence and Caro kept her peace. She knew the signs. When Laney shut up and got all stiff, she wasn't in the mood to talk or negotiate. The last time she'd been that upset, short of Grant, had been in college. It had taken a good week of letting her stew and silently process before she confessed to having a change in her major, from pre–med to journalism.

After several minutes of quiet and road noise, Laney took an exit off the interstate and onto a smaller road. She found a park and a parking space near a wide expanse of green. She shoved the car into park and faced Caro.

"What do you mean, you'll never have a relationship or commitment?" No wonder she wanted to go to somewhere private; her volume wouldn't have been tolerated in the ice cream shop.

"Look at the facts, Laney. I date men, but I rarely get past the first month in a relationship."

"Have you ever wondered why that is?"

Caro snorted a laugh. "I know why. The guy sees and expects some classic woman like Grace Kelly but gets me instead."

Laney pounded the car steering wheel in frustration. "You're more than a pretty face, Caro!"

"I know that and you know that. Unfortunately, every man I've ever dated apparently doesn't care what's under the façade. They want the trophy."

"There's someone out there that'll see you for who you really are." Laney eyed Caro in silence then continued, "You were interested in the guy at the garage, right?"

"Yeah," Caro drawled in caution.

"So go after him. You never know."

"It wouldn't do any good, he wasn't interested."

"Caro, there isn't a man alive that isn't interested in you. Besides, you told me something a few months ago and I'm going to give it right back to you." Laney shifted to face Caro, her expression earnest. "If you want a relationship, you can have one."

"If I remember my advice to you, it was go get your guy. I don't have a guy in mind right now." *Liar.*

"So, just go into the singles' events with an attitude that you'll make an effort to be nice."

"I'm always nice." Caro shot back, affronted.

"And stay nice. Don't insult the guy on your first date."

"Couldn't help it, Franklin left himself wide open." Caro's grin turned sly as she thought of Franklin's face.

Laney smiled back, then chuckled. "Okay, be nice to the normal, nonegocentric guys, okay?"

"Fine. Now, can we go back to the office?"

"You're feeling better?"

"Yeah, pity party is over for the month. I found some information about some special interest singles' groups."

"What kind of groups are there?"

"Pretty much any kind you want. If you have a hobby or predilection, there's a group out there for you."

Laney started the car and headed back toward the office. "Anything that appealed to you?"

"Some. I thought I'd try the sporting singles' group, the singles for charity, and a group that offers board games and that sort of stuff—"

"Board games? You looking for the geriatric set?"

Caro stuck her tongue out at her friend. "You may not see yourself having a good time playing Trivial Pursuit or Balderdash with a group of people, but a lot of singles our age enjoy an evening like that. Besides, I wanted a cross section of singles' groups, other than the faith based ones. I think I've done a good job."

"You're right, it is a good sample. How do you meet up with these guys?"

"All of them meet in groups, some as small as three or four. Safety in numbers, but no guarantee you'll pair up."

"Any of them meeting soon?"

"Yeah, the game group is meeting in a week and the charity group is building a house this weekend. I'm going to go to both of the meetings, and see what I can see."

"I wonder if we need to reinstitute the shadow." Laney murmured.

"No. No way, no how. You gave me a choice when I took on this thing and I'm not going to have a shadow on all my dates, like you did." Caro shook her finger at Laney.

"It turned out good for me." Laney's face took on a rosy hue. Her shadow, Grant turned out to be more attracted to her than he'd ever imagined.

"Yeah, but we know about lightning striking twice, don't we? No, I'll just look for my man the old fashioned way. By getting out there and meeting as many single guys in as little time as possible."

"And write articles about it. Yeah, traditional." Laney shot back.

Chapter Four

Gus peered out of the window of the truck as he neared the construction site and maneuvered into a parking place along the street. The Atlanta neighborhood wasn't the best, but the neat one and two story brick houses that lined it made up for the cracks in the sidewalk and narrow streets.

The house being renovated this weekend was over eighty years old and, a month ago, had looked every bit of its age. Now, with a little more money and a lot of elbow grease provided by volunteers, a new family would move into the abandoned house, putting another brick in the solid neighborhood's comeback.

Gus locked the truck and then rounded the bed. He unlocked the bed tool box, pulled out his tool belt, and then retrieved a large water container.

Several people mingled around the house. What groups had volunteered this weekend? He tried to pull out the information but couldn't remember whether it was a church youth group, a neighborhood VFW, or a garden club. *Don't let it be the garden club.* They were great at mulching, planting and digging but the ladies couldn't handle a hammer worth squat.

A knot of men gathered at the bottom of the front porch, looking at something or talking. Gus approached them, ready to find out who the job boss was for the day when he noticed a blonde head in the center of the huddle. A laugh drifted over their heads toward him and he grinned.

A woman. That explained the crowd, and judging by the size of the group, an attractive one. Nothing threw a clinker in a workday schedule like a pretty woman on the site.

"Hey, guys. Anyone know what's on tap for today?"

A head or two turned toward him, then a man separated from the pack and headed toward Gus, his hand outstretched.

"Hey, Gus. We're just waiting for the rest of the groups to show up and we'll get started on the roof and the interior finishing work."

"Who's volunteering today?" Gus ambled up the sidewalk with Bill, the head of a construction company in the area.

"Let's see. There's a group that does charity work

once a month and a group from the AME church down the road. With the individual volunteers, like you, that'll put us near thirty people, along with the owners."

"Great. We'll get some work done, that way."

Bill came to a stop at the edge of the clutch of men and woman, turned to face Gus with his arms crossed at his chest. "Ready to work, huh?"

"Yeah. Need to work off some steam." Gus didn't share that the excess energy came from memories of a certain lady. He couldn't shake the feeling he'd missed out on something pretty special when he thought of her.

"Let's get to it, then." Bill plunged into the center of the group and broke it up, leaving Gus staring in shock at the woman in the midst of it all.

"What are you doing here?"

"Well, hello to you too, and thank you for welcoming me so warmly." Caroline Paul bit out her greeting with a clearly false smile, but Gus thought he saw hurt in her eyes.

"Sorry. I just didn't expect to see you here, in that." He waved his hand first toward the slightly run-down area and then toward her in her neat figure, clad in white t-shirt and jeans. The top, emblazoned with a ten K race he'd participated in last fall, looked a lot better on her than on him when he wore its partner.

"In this? I wear jeans all the time," she bristled.

"I'm sure you do." *In the comfort of your home.*

She looked ready to continue sparring with him when a middle aged woman approached her. "Caroline, they're assigning jobs inside. You want to come in and see what suits you?"

"Sure," Caroline smiled at the woman then cast a sharp glance toward Gus. "I'm finished here."

Gus followed the two as they climbed the cinder block steps to the porch. His every instinct said go after her, yet, his last experience with a woman as sophisticated and stylish as her had burned him. Still, he'd depended on his gut in the past and now his gut urged him to get to know her better.

Everything he'd done in the past, he'd put all of his effort into. And he'd taken a lot of chances in the past, in his business life as well as personal. Now, as he eyed the trim figure ahead of him, he realized, he was about to take another risk. And this one could have great payoffs.

The tasks available for the morning were varied. There were jobs typical of the construction business, shingling, installing drywall and finishing work. Then there was the lighter work, the work most of the younger set and women did, the cleanup, fetch and carrying and the water boys. Gus was used to doing shingling and installing drywall, so he lounged near the back of the room, waiting for the other jobs to be assigned.

"Gus, you going to be up or down?" Bill yelled over the buzz of conversation.

Gus noticed Caroline wandering over to the nail boxes and finger one of the finishing nails. Hoping he was right, he answered Bill, "I'll take down this morning, maybe go up later." She probably wouldn't last more than a couple of hours anyway.

"Okay, folks, let's get started. For those of you working on the drywall and finishing, that's in the four bedrooms. The drywall is in the hallway, remember to use your back right. Your job boss will be Gus. He's experienced at this sort of thing, so ask if you need help." Bill ended his speech with a wave and disappeared outside.

Gus ambled over to the nail boxes. As he approached, Caroline turned and eyed him, her expression anxious. "You're in charge of the finishing crew?"

"Yep. You on it?"

"Uh huh." She gripped the carpenter's apron in her hands tighter. Did she want to spend the day around him, sensing him? And having him judge her abilities and finding her wanting? Or did she give up and leave?

No. She wouldn't leave simply because she was uncomfortable around him. There was a writing assignment she had to finish, after all. And she knew what she was doing, too.

The task she'd been assigned was to hold the drywall being cut to fit, then stabilizing it for the person nailing it to the studs in the wall. She had work gloves, nails and a hammer, but wasn't expected to use the hammer. And the nails were to be handed to the "real worker." At the time she'd been assigned the task, Caro felt sure it suited her. Now, as she sensed Gus's misgivings about her, she wished she'd volunteered for something more exciting, like sawing. Well, if she had the assignment of being a helper, then help she would.

"I'm Caroline Paul, by the way." She tied her apron on and stepped up to hold her hand out for a handshake.

He accepted her hand in his larger one, firm and sure. "I know. Gus Hill. Let's start in the master bedroom."

Gus glanced over at Caroline as he hammered another row of nails in the piece of drywall. They'd been at work for three hours and a fine layer of white gypsum covered both of them from the sawed material. She'd answered his questions with a pleasant, light voice, all the while focused on her job.

He had to admit it, she'd surprised him. She didn't complain of her shoulders aching, though they had to, from holding them over her head for hours. She didn't gripe about the humid warmth, the occasional bug that pestered them or the constant din of noise in the background.

"Let's take a break." He rolled his shoulders in an effort to loosen them.

"Okay." She slowly lowered her own arms, further indicating her discomfort.

"Come on over and have a drink." Gus sank onto the floor, disregarding the saw dust and dirt. When she did the same, his opinion of her raised yet another notch.

He pulled off his work gloves then reached into the cooler beside him and extracted two bottles of water. After he passed her one he twisted the cap of his and took a generous drink.

She laid her own gloves beside her on the floor then drank from her bottle. After a long drink, she lowered the bottle to glance around the room. "We'll finish the drywalling today, won't we?"

"In this room, yeah. Don't know what's going on in the other rooms." He rested his head against the wall behind him, then swiveled his neck toward her. "You're doing a good job, Caroline."

"Much to your surprise?" She turned her gaze on him, her light green eyes steady.

"Sorry about that." She didn't bother to hide her surprise and he grinned. "You have a certain look, lady. Can't help it, I made a judgment. And I was wrong."

"You're basing the change of heart on the fact that I can hold a board up for you?"

"No. I'm basing the change of heart on the fact that you've spent three hours holding boards, getting sawdust and gypsum dust all over you, and I'll bet your arms hurt like the dickens."

"I don't think I'll raise them again." She moaned and tried unsuccessfully to roll her shoulders.

"Tell you what. We finish this today and I'll treat you to a dinner and a shoulder rub. Deal?"

She looked at him for several seconds then with a smile and nod, assented.

Caro rushed through a shower and changed into a simple T–shirt and jeans. After drying and running a brush through her hair she jogged to the living room and grabbed her purse then looked at the clock.

"A record." She murmured, giggling. Gus had given her an hour to change out of the sweaty, dirty clothes she'd worked in all day and she had twenty minutes to spare. After she thought a minute she wheeled around and reentered the bathroom.

She peered into the vanity mirror, shocked. She'd forgotten her makeup! "I never forget my makeup." Since she'd sneaked mascara at fourteen, she'd not forgotten to put makeup on before leaving the house. This morning, when her expectations had been to fetch and carry in a dusty house, she'd put on makeup.

"I've lost my mind." She grabbed her makeup bag and set to work. In ten minutes, she had a light, natural look that she'd spent her adult life perfecting. *Now* she was ready for her date.

As she returned to the living room of her apartment, the doorbell rang. With uncharacteristic jitters in her stomach, Caro opened the door. *Holy cow.*

Gus stood on the threshold, clad in jeans, a polo shirt, open to the second button, and a worn leather jacket. Every high school fantasy of a bad boy she'd had came to the forefront as she invited him in.

"Ready for dinner?" His smile warmed her through and through.

"Um–hmm. I just need a sweater." She reached into the coat closet for a light cardigan. Gus reached around her and took the garment from her hands.

"Let me." He held the sweater ready for her to slip her arms into and as Caro donned it, she felt the tingling warmth of his hands on her shoulders.

"Arms still aching?" He cupped her shoulders and squeezed gently.

"A bit," She murmured.

He intensified the pressure of his hands as he rubbed out some of the tension she'd worked into her muscles. Caro stood, her head bent, barely suppressing a groan at the sensations.

A moment later, Gus stepped away from her and removed his hands from her shoulders. Caro glanced over her shoulder at him and was greeted by a smile. "Sorry. Not something to do on a first date, huh?"

"Oh, I don't know. You made a pretty good impression." She grinned and rolled her shoulders.

His smile widened and with a gesture, he ushered her out the door.

Caro glanced around the restaurant before leveling her green eyed gaze on Gus. "I've never been here before."

"I've known the guy who owns it for years. We went to school together."

She didn't look put–out that he'd brought her to a barbeque joint in midtown. Not the type of place a woman like her would go to on a date, he bet. "Do you like barbeque?"

"Yeah, I do, but I don't have a lot of opportunities to get good pulled barbeque."

"Travis said you work at a newspaper. What do you do?" Gus sipped his iced tea as he watched her hands. Pale and thin, they looked like artist's hands. But she fidgeted. She'd pulled a packet of artificial sweetener out of the container on the table and ran it through her hands, lightly scoring it with her nails.

"I'm a society reporter." She grinned at his look and Gus was sure he'd not been able to hide his aversion. "It's not as gross as it sounds. I just go to fancy parties and drop the names my editor insists I drop."

"I've read those columns." *And been targeted by them.* "You like the lifestyle?"

Caro's grin turned into a laugh. "You've seen my car. I don't live the lifestyle. I have some of the clothes because I go to model sales. And as far as the parties and so on, I hate them. I'd much rather be in a barbeque place listening to blues than having rubber chicken at yet another charity ball."

Was she as good as she sounded? He eyed her as she sipped her iced tea and took in the restaurant's ambiance. The place, built in the 1930's, was housed in an old residence, and had the rabbit warren rooms that personified a family owned business. The usual clientele consisted of families and middle class individuals. That Gus was on a first name basis with the owners said a lot.

"So you don't like the glitzy lifestyle." He eyed her with what he hoped looked like belief.

"Nope. I'm a UGA fan, like going to the beach if I can afford it for vacation and love eating corn dogs at the fair every year." She smiled, as if she knew he wasn't quite buying it.

"And the house building?" He sipped his beer.

"Today was my first time. I enjoyed it though. It's

nice seeing results from your work, especially when it's worth while."

"Yeah. You did a good job today. What brought you out?"

"I had an assignment for my paper." Caro fiddled with her iced tea as she avoided meeting Gus's eye gaze.

"On the community work crew?"

"Sort of." Should she tell him now? Now, that she truly enjoyed being on a date with a man?

"Sort of?"

"Not really. In addition to the society column I'm doing a column on being single in the area." Great. Now he'd make an excuse and the date'd be over.

"A singles' column?"

"Um hmm. I cover the different singles' events in the city, the opportunities singles have to meet and socialize."

He leaned back in his chair as his gaze turned assessing. "I heard about the column, on a radio program last year."

"I didn't have the byline last year, my friends did. And the column's changed a bit this year."

"How?"

It felt a bit like being cross examined, Caro thought. But, what the hey. "Last year Laney went out on dates and was trailed by her partner, Grant. It was more personal, I guess. This year, I'm concentrating on looking at opportunities for singles, such as volunteer opportunities, specialty clubs, that sort of thing. Hence, the house project this morning."

Gus nodded. Caro hid a smile as she watched him relax into his seat. No, she wouldn't be writing about their date, though she would highlight the house project.

"What about you? Besides the garage and Travis, of course, I don't know much about you." She urged.

"That's about it. I like fishing, Nascar, and Georgia football. And I volunteer at building houses. I'm a pretty simple guy."

Somehow, Caro didn't believe that.

The rest of the evening passed quickly, in Caro's eyes. When she checked her watch, she noticed that over three hours passed as she and Gus ate ribs, corn, potatoes, and dessert. But when she thought of the night, she remembered talking about football, working at the house, and so many other things. And not once did she get bored.

The evening ended with Gus taking her to the door, his hand resting lightly on her waist. She retrieved the key from her purse then turned to him.

"I had fun."

"Me too." He sounded a bit surprised.

"Goodnight." She tamped down the disappointment that he hadn't even talked about going out again.

"Caroline." He took a step toward her, putting him within a hair's breadth of touching her.

"Hmm?"

"I'll call you." His head lowered slightly.

"'Kay," she murmured.

His lips brushed hers, firm and warm. Caro leaned forward to increase the contact. After a sweet, time-stopping moment, he withdrew and with a smile, took her key and unlocked the door for her. He reached around her, opened the door and glanced another kiss on her mouth.

She entered her apartment and, after closing and locking the door, leaned against it with a smile. Finally, a man who was as straightforward as he was a good kisser.

Chapter Five

"I'm going to kill Grant." Laney dug into the bag of cheese puffs.

Caro grinned at her friend. Whenever Laney was nervous or had a flash of insight, she became ravenous. When she'd called Caro and told her she was on her way over, Caro had run to the grocery and stocked up on the forbidden foods. Cheese puffs, full fat ice cream, and Choco Blokos, an obsence mixture of chocolate, vanilla cream filling and chocolate icing that passed as luncheon cakes. Laney usually worked her way through all three items when depressed or excited.

"What happened?" Caro leaned back into her sofa and folded her legs underneath her.

"He volunteered us to host a single's event in

Tampa next month. One of the singles' fast dates." Laney crammed more puffs in her mouth.

"So, what's wrong with that? You did that as part of *The Single Life* column. It's old hat for you."

"It's also excruciating. Imagine having to encourage twenty or so people who hate being there to be nice to each other. I'm going to make him pay." Laney drawled the last word and grinned her patented evil grin. Caro chuckled. The evil grin meant practical jokes.

"What are you going to do?" Maybe she'd warn Grant ahead of time. Her best friend's boyfriend was really a good guy.

"Not sure yet. But something good. So, what's up with you? How was the house building project?"

Caro's grin widened. "It was good. I'm glad you had the idea."

Laney eyed Caro for a minute then sat upright. "You met a guy, didn't you?"

"Uh–huh."

"Cute?"

"Uh–huh."

Laney huffed. "Give. Now."

"His name is Gus and—"

"Gus? Wasn't that that garage guy's name?"

"Uh–huh." If she smiled any wider Caro was convinced her mouth would hurt for hours afterwards.

Laney scooted from her chair and plopped down beside Caro. "I want details, and I want them now."

Caro filled her in on the house project and Gus. As she reminisced, Caro realized she wanted Gus to call her. For the first time in a long time, she wanted a guy to ask her out for a second time.

"And you know the best part? I really think he's on the up and up. No fish stories, no lies, no made up professions."

"And you think he's a hunk. It gets better and better." Laney's chuckle grew into a laugh.

The giddy feeling she'd felt yesterday returned with a vengeance and Caro joined in her friend's laughter.

"Why are we laughing?" Caro stopped long enough to take a breath as her stomach started to hurt.

"No reason, honey. No reason at all." Laney chortled and doubled over.

"What's she like?" Travis bit into the thick burger with delight.

"Pretty much like she was at the garage."

"Okay. Gorgeous, well mannered, too good for a mug like you."

"Yeah. But the kicker is, she's a reporter." Gus glanced around the fast food restaurant, his mood unsettled.

"Yeah, she told me that when she stopped by before. And I told you." Travis's hand wavered as he reached for his soda.

"A reporter, as in digging up facts about people. She was doing a story on the singles scene." Gus pushed the burger he'd been eating away, not hungry anymore.

"Bummer. She seemed to like you at the garage."

Gus leaned back and stared into space. Caro did like him and the feeling was mutual.

"Hey, pal. Did you?" Travis's voice brought him back.

"Did I what?"

"Did you ask her out again or are you cutting your losses?"

"I took her number."

"So you're going for it? Even considering the stuff you've had to put up with from the press?" Travis abandoned his burger too.

"I need to think about it. I might." Gus checked his watch and reached for his wallet. "Listen, I need to go. I have a meeting in twenty minutes. I'll stop by the garage this evening and check out the Grand Am's exhaust."

"Gotcha. I'm going to finish this before I get back." Travis turned his attention to his burger and Gus headed toward the cash register.

Gus settled his bill and retreated to his car. As he

merged into the traffic heading toward the city, he did what he did best. He went through the pros and cons of seeing Caro again.

Pros, she was the first woman he'd met in too long that he actually felt a tremor of attraction for, and she apparently returned the feeling. She sounded down to earth and wielded a decent hammer, he grinned to himself. And she was the most beautiful woman he'd ever met.

Okay, now for the cons. She was a reporter. For the *Globe*.

So far the negatives outweighed the positive aspects of dating Caro. Still, Gus picked up his cell phone and punched in the number he'd rather not admit he'd memorized.

The phone rang the requisite four times, then a voice message came through. "Hello. This is Caroline. I'm unavailable right now, so leave a message and I'll call you back."

Nice. Not flashy. Gus left a short message and disconnected.

So much for the cons. He'd always believed in taking risks.

He pulled his car into the parking lot to a business park and entered a nondescript building. The receptionist greeted him with a smile and he strode down the hall toward a bank of office doors. As he neared the middle of the hall a woman exited the office.

The Single File

"Mr. Hill. I didn't know you were coming into the office today," she gushed.

"Really? I had the appointment on my calendar, Ms. French." And she had on the dress he suspected he'd complimented her on last week.

"Well, I'm glad to see you. We just don't see you often enough anymore." She sashayed past him and Gus shook his head.

His office was neat and orderly, just the way he'd left it a few hours before. A file rested squarely on the gleaming wood surface, ready for his review. The proposal for another garage in South Carolina would expand his business into the fourth state in the region. He quickly scanned the proposal and then placed the call to the owner's realty agent.

Two hours later and he was the proud owner of a plot of land outside of Columbia. Four acres would be plenty of room to expand if the garage took off as expected.

Gus took another two hours to clear up paperwork before he left. Somehow the work took longer than it had in years past, and wasn't nearly the challenge it had been.

On the way to the garage, his real avocation, he reviewed his day. Financially, it was a success, he'd acquired another property for Hill's Garage Works and it'd be a success. He'd make sure of it.

But over the years, the acquisitions had become

more routine, the management a bore. The only thing he looked forward to anymore was the time he spent in his old, his first garage, alongside Travis.

A cold drink and his overalls awaited him at the garage. Travis was singing along with the country song about a Mercury as he thumbed through a supply catalog.

Gus sipped his drink and leaned against the door. "What are you looking for?"

"A set of headlights. The ones on the Grand Am are shot."

"Literally. I heard two punks shot out all the lights with BB guns."

Travis grinned. "Hey, that's what you get when you buy the car from the junk yard."

"I got a good deal." Gus approached the car and ran a hand along the spotty exterior. After they finished the engine rebuild, he'd start on the body. In a few months' time, he'd have a prime car.

"How'd the deal go?" Travis wheeled around to the front of the car, pulled a screwdriver from his shirt pocket and started loosening the headlight remains.

"Fine. I signed the offer on the place in Columbia." He popped the hood and lifted it before glancing over. "The offer's still on the table."

Travis dropped the glass form onto the canvas lap robe he protected his legs with. He shifted a bit to the turn signal lights and started unscrewing them. "I thought you sent the offer to the guy's attorneys in Columbia."

"Not the property. Your job."

"I have a job right here." Travis didn't look away from his task.

"But if you want—"

Travis held up a hand. "I don't. Look, both of us always wanted to own a garage and we have it. I'm satisfied right here." He turned to the car again, and then looked up at Gus. "It wasn't your fault."

Gus shrugged, uncomfortable with the direction of the conversation. "Well, if you're sure."

"I am. I see what crap you have to put up with, the suits and all that. I'd rather be elbow deep in grease than sit in on a contract meeting."

"Yeah, so would I." Gus grumbled and smiled at Travis' laughter.

They worked for a few minutes, the only sounds the clinking of glass and metal and the sounds of the radio in the background. When the sound of a car horn interrupted them, Gus straightened and wiped his hands as he headed to the workbench. He picked up his cell phone and flipped it open. "Gus Hill."

"Hi, it's Caroline."

"Hey. What are you doing Thursday night?" He grinned, way too pleased she'd called him back. In the background, he heard the sound of Travis' chair, the soft whirr of wheels against the concrete floor.

A soft silence followed his question then her voice drifted through the air. "Nothing."

"Have dinner with me."

"Dinner?"

"Yeah, we'll eat, talk, maybe take in a movie."

"Okay."

"I'll pick you up at seven, okay?"

"I'm looking forward to it."

He hung up, reluctant to end the conversation but also hesitant to conduct a private conversation in front of Travis. And that in itself was worrisome.

He tossed the phone onto the counter top and turned. Travis sat, crushed glass in his lap, and a grin on his face.

"Man, you got it bad."

"I don't even know her."

"You don't have to know her. You just have to want to."

And whether he'd admit it to his friend or not, Gus definitely wanted to know Caroline Paul.

Chapter Six

Caro stared at the blank screen in front of her, lost in thought. Gus's call the evening before created more giddiness, anxiety, and even fear in her than ever. No guy had brought out feelings like this before. His gaze, intent, and focus during dinner the other night, after the house project, increased the knowledge he was as interested in her as she was him. If she could just be sure it wasn't just her good looks that attracted him, but the whole person—the true Caro.

She finally gave up writing in the office and fled for wider spaces. With a lame excuse she headed home to her running shoes. She quickly donned sweats, a T–shirt, and her sneakers, then jogged onto the street in front of her apartment building. She ran a couple of blocks to a community park and entered the jogging trail that ran along three miles of dips, valleys, and level strips. By then she had hit her stride and could run, her body in automatic while her mind addressed the problem. And in a snap, the problem was Gus Hill.

That he was gorgeous was a given. Brown hair shot through with blond streaks, warm topaz eyes, and a body that implied his muscles weren't from working out in a gym but from pick-up ball games, lifting whatever men lifted in garages, and sheer hard work.

Did she take the chance on Gus? Caro pushed up a hill with a vengeance. He'd break her heart if he didn't pan out, that was as sure as the handsome topaz eyes.

As she rounded the top of the hill her cell phone vibrated against her hip. She pulled it from the inside pocket of her sweats and flipped it open.

"Lo." Her breath was a bit short from the hill but she could still talk, sort of.

"Caroline, is something wrong?"

Lord, Mom. "Hey. No, just running. What's up?"

"I wish you'd find some other way to exercise. A club is such a nice place to meet men."

"I don't like gyms, Mom. I like to run outside." Even if it didn't get her away from nagging. But it was her own fault, she should have checked the number on the phone display first.

"Well, it worked for me, you know. I met Henry there."

"Henry?" Caro slowed in response to the strange name. "Who's Henry?"

"That's another reason I'm calling you. I'm engaged!" Her mother finished with a squeal that belonged to a high school cheerleader, rather than a woman in her fifties and on the outside of her second marriage.

"Congratulations. What's up with Frank?" Her stepfather, bless his heart, had hung in there for three years since the divorce.

"Honey, you should see him. He's losing his hair and gained at least twenty pounds. He looks so *old*."

"He's two years younger than you are, Mom." And not fighting time.

"But I don't look my age and neither do you. And Henry is six years younger than me. It's so inspiring."

"Inspiring?" *As in Botox and lipo inspiring?* Caro thought to herself.

"To keep looking young, silly. Well, I've got to go. I've got an appointment to sell a piece of commercial property on Peachtree. I'll call you in a couple of days and we'll get together for lunch, okay?"

"Su—" The other line disconnected before Caro

could finish. With a sigh she flipped the phone closed and resumed her run.

With a family history like hers, what were the chances she'd even have a relationship that lasted longer than her mom's courtship? Slim and none.

That evening, Gus carried the sack of take out burgers and the latest issue of *The Globe* to the recliner centered in the middle of his living room. It was the classic bachelor pad, replete with a big screen tv, a couple of game systems he resorted to in bad weather and during sleepless nights, and worn but comfortable furniture.

The house, situated in a wooded lot near his parents' old house, remained as it had been when he built it ten years ago. Cedar siding, a wooded deck and bedrooms that remained largely empty, it housed him but didn't really feel like a home. And probably wouldn't until he filled it with a wife and kids.

He opened the newspaper and ignored the headlines; he already knew the world was going to pot from the news on the radio. He'd get to it, he always did. He ignored the sports section, out of character for him, and turned to the lifestyle section.

There it was. *The Single Life.* He scanned the body of the short column then returned to it to read it more closely. As he started the column read-through, in the back of his mind he realized he was making a crucial decision.

> When you're looking for someone special in your life, you might find yourself doing some strange things. In my life, I've gone to parties that featured kegs more than any other item, I've been fixed up and I've even gone to concerts, boxing matches, and bass tournaments (that I didn't get to fish in) to meet and get to know that special guy. Well, this time, I hit the jackpot. I went to a volunteer event sponsored by a local singles' group. I got to meet a lot of great people who spend valuable personal time giving to others. And I got to spend time getting to know the business end of a hammer helping build a house. And I met a guy. A great guy, a guy I want to get to know more.

He grinned openly as he ended the column. He'd been the only guy she'd gotten to really meet on the project, he'd made sure of that. He glanced through the rest of the section and scanned her society column. It consisted of a review of a bridal shower of all things, with the bride and groom, their families and their families' families all mentioned. It seemed to be more of an advertisement for the genealogy of the principal parties than a news column. But then, maybe all society columns were like that. This evening was the first time he'd remembered ever reading the blasted thing.

One thing was sure, though. He'd go for it with Caroline.

As soon as she arrived at work the next morning, Caro dialed the phone number on the ad for Sporty Singles. The web page had a tentative date for the rafting trip and she needed more information. Such as did they take total beginners?

"Hi, you've reached the Sporty Singles." The message droned on and she waited to ask her questions and return phone numbers. When she hung up at least she had a firm date for the trip. The next Saturday, she'd be on the river, unless she was *in* it.

She glanced at her calendar on the desk for her list. Next item, the game night singles, then the— matchmaker?

"Whoa. That one was covered when Laney did the column." She muttered to herself and tried to pull her mind together. Finally, with a groan at her less than accurate memory, she left her desk and headed to Grant and Laney's area.

The desks sat at angles, kind of like the couple, she thought. Touching and together, but still unique. Laney's desk, the military reject from her tiny cubicle area, held piles of papers; tiny plastic figurines rested atop her computer monitor, and she spun around on what looked like a new desk chair.

Grant lounged in his own chair, smiling at Laney, his hands cocked back behind his head. Behind him, his desk had some piles but they looked collated and organized, and his monitor held nothing more than a screensaver of his favorite team, the Braves.

"Hey, guys. I had a question." Caro approached the couple, interrupting their banter about the expense of the chair.

"Did you see my new chair? Isn't it cool?" Laney kicked out her foot and took another spin.

Caro murmured her appreciation of the ubiquitous office chair and Grant turned his grin toward her. "At least she won't fall out of it if she tries to lean back."

Laney had accumulated all the office rejects and loved them with a passion, even the forties' metal desk. But her old chair had a swivel and dump feature she hadn't appreciated, nor had anyone who made the mistake of sitting in it.

"It's great. Now, I really need to pick your brains." Caro perched on the edge of Laney's desk.

"Such as they are. Go ahead." Laney came to a standstill then and focused on Caro.

"I'm trying to contact the singles' groups we talked about. I've contacted the charity group, it was great by the way." Caro ignored Laney's snicker.

"And I've called about the sports singles' group and the game night group. But, I have the matchmaker on my list and I can't remember what we were going to do with that. After all, you covered that last time."

"We did. But that was one of the columns that got the most letters and comments online. We wanted to do a followup." Laney cast an apologetic glance toward Caro.

"So, I need to get in touch with your matchmaker?" Caro swallowed the lump in her throat at the thought.

"Yeah. Here's the business card we had. Myra was a kick. You'll like her." Clearly Grant didn't remember the panic Laney had felt every time she had to meet a stranger, but Caro did.

"And it's really not bad. The matchmaker is pretty good." If he'd meant to encourage her, Grant needed to give it a little more effort.

Caro accepted the card. "Right. Okay, I'll go call now."

"Hey, we're going to the deli for lunch. Want to come?" Laney called behind her as Caro headed back toward her work area.

"No. If I don't do this, I might chicken out."

"'Kay. Call me tonight."

Caro lifted a hand in acknowledgement without turning.

She reseated herself and with a heave, dialed the

number on the business card. Myra Lange, Matchmaker Extraordinare. Well, heck, she'd done worse things to meet a guy.

After a couple of rings a timid voice sounded. "Hello?"

"Hi. I'm calling for Myra Lange about the matchmaking service."

"She's retired from matchmaking. Moved to Florida."

Great. "So, no one's covering her business?"

After a long pause, a sigh sounded over the phone. "No, I'm taking over the business."

Well, shoot. "Oh. Okay, I need to make an appointment, I guess."

"Can you come by at six this evening?"

"Yeah. Could you give me the address?"

Caro jotted down an address with some reluctance.

Five hours later, Caro knocked on the door of the Victorian house on the corner of a street she'd expect to see in New England rather than downtown Atlanta. She tamped down the anxiety that bubbled up in her stomach, threatening to choke her. This couldn't be that hard.

A slight woman, little more than a teenager, really, opened the door and smiled a hesitant grin. "Caroline?"

"Yes."

"I'm Miriah. Come in, please."

Caro followed Miriah into the nineteenth century. The house was furnished in period pieces, including horsehair chairs and sofas, a dial phone (at least that was twentieth century) and a rolltop desk. Caro perched on the sofa and eyed her hostess.

Miriah looked totally at home in the house, but not with her profession. A flush darkened her cheeks and she looked as uncomfortable as Caro felt.

"I'm not sure what we're supposed to do." Caro confessed.

"To be honest, neither am I," Miriah sighed.

"You're not?"

Miriah shook her head and Caro's anxiety paradoxically lessened. "Do you mind me asking you why?"

"Why I'm a matchmaker? My aunt wanted to move to Florida with her new husband. She needed someone to take over the family house and business. And I'm the one she chose to do it." Miriah finished with a shrug.

"Okay. Didn't your aunt leave, I don't know, instructions or something?" Caro shifted on the uncomfortable couch. Why was she still here? It was the perfect excuse to go back home. But Miriah, complete with deer in the headlights eyes, curly blonde hair and a lost expression, reminded her of the little sister she never had.

Miriah brightened and nodded. "Yes, she did. Wait

a minute." She hopped up and sprinted to the desk, which she opened. A computer monitor rested inside, the comforting presence of modernity. Tucked alongside the monitor was a manilla envelope. Miriah returned to the chair and rummaged in the folder then grinned. "I studied these when she first gave them to me, but it's been a while." She flipped through several pages then glanced up at Caro with a quirk in her smile. "Okay, we can do this."

Caro smiled in encouragement and proceeded to answer a ton of questions about her likes, her history and the things she couldn't abide in a man. At the end of the interview, Miriah leaned back with a sigh.

"I think I'll be able to get something in line for you by the end of the week. Or someone, I should say."

"Miriah, is this your only job?" If it was, Caro had doubts the poor girl would be able to afford food for a week.

Miriah chuckled. "No, thank God. I'm an antiques dealer and clothes designer."

Caro cast a critical eye at the other woman's outfit. The skirt she wore with a lightweight sweater was bohemian in design, but made of rich fabric, full of color and very complementary. "Did you design your skirt?"

"Yes." Miriah shrugged, a sheepish smile on her

face, "So far, I'm the most reliable customer I've got. I earn my money through the antiques dealing, but hope to get established in design eventually."

"I'm sure you'll do it, if the outfit you're wearing is any indication." Caro smiled encouragingly. "Well, I'll look forward to hearing from you about the matchmaking."

As Caro drove to her apartment, she pulled on the headset to her cell phone and dialed Laney. When Laney answered, she blasted her friend.

"What did you get me into?"

"Huh?"

"The matchmaker." Caro glanced into the rearview mirror and merged into traffic on the interstate.

"Myra? She's a neat old lady."

"No. Miriah, her niece. A very nice *young* lady, who happens to be a designer and antiques dealer, but has no clue how to be a matchmaker."

"Miriah? I thought Myra—"

"Nope. Miriah. Myra got married and moved to Florida."

"Well, how hard can matchmaking be?" Laney answered flippantly.

"Apparently, not so much for you. You've already got a guy."

"And you might have one. Maybe two." Laney shot back. "Have you heard back from Gus?"

"Yeah. We're going out tomorrow night."

"Yes!" By her tone, Caro imagined Laney thrusting her fist into the air in triumph.

"Don't get so worked up, it's only the second date."

"And a second date is a lot better than you've done since you started the column, and before, if you want the truth."

"Don't remind me. But still, I don't want to get too excited about it. It may not work out, after all."

"Hey, kid, I'm going to give you the same advice that you gave me. If you want the guy, go for it. Throw caution to the wind, go for the gold—"

"Give it one for the Gipper? God, give me a break."

"Well, heck Caro. Do it. You like the guy, you know it, I know it, and Grant knows it. So do it."

"I'm hitting traffic, got to go." Caro ended the call in exasperation. Just because Laney was happy and giddy in love didn't mean everyone could be that way. After all, Gus was just a nice guy that she wanted to date. And the evening ahead would tell the tale whether a second date would work with him.

"How's the steak?" Gus's deep baritone rumbled across the table and Caro lifted her head to smile at him.

"It's great. One of the better filets I've had." She eyed the rustic restaurant, "This is a nice place."

"It's a favorite of mine. Quiet, small and doesn't keep up with the Joneses."

"You have a lot of favorite restaurants, don't you?" She teased.

Gus grinned, his face lighted by the candle in the glass holder. "Yeah. I don't eat in much. And I've gotten good at ferreting out the good places and thinning the over priced, over-publicized ones."

Caro smiled as she cut into her food. "If you've found the secret, you could become the most popular guy in Atlanta, maybe even Georgia."

"Maybe with the customers, but not the restaurateurs," he shot back and they shared a laugh.

Caro leaned back and sipped her wine. "Tell me about Travis."

"We went to school together, both liked fooling around with cars. We got our first jobs at the same garage after high school and when the opportunity came to buy the place, we took it."

"And the wheelchair?" She wondered if she was pressing too far.

Gus's expression flattened. "He had an accident when we were working on an engine rebuild. The scaffolding fell and crushed his spine. He's been in the chair for four years, now."

"I'm sorry. He seems like a great guy." Caro reached out and touched the back of his hand as it rested on the table beside his plate.

"He is. And he likes you." Gus's face lightened a bit with his remark.

"What's not to like?" she teased.

"Not a thing that I've found." His eyes burned brighter.

Suddenly her steak held less appeal than this man.

"I read your column."

"Boring as dirt, I know."

"Not really. I thought the idea of looking for new activities for singles was a nice touch."

"Oh, the singles column." Oh cripes. She'd mentioned meeting him in that column.

"Yeah. And I agree. You meet very nice people in the construction zone."

Caro noticed when he smiled one side of his mouth tilted a bit more than the other, lending a very lazy, warm look to his grin.

"I've lined up another outing with a sporting group."

"Sounds like dog show stuff."

"Ha ha. It's a singles' group that does different sports on the weekends, mostly. I'm going on a rafting trip this Saturday." On impulse she added, "Want to join me?"

"Rafting? Yeah, I would." He took a drink from his beer.

"Great. I'll check on the details and call you tomorrow, okay?"

"Good enough. So, what's up after dinner? Are you in the mood for a movie or a walk in the moonlight?"

Oh, the temptation for a walk, but Caro still wanted to play it safe. "A movie sounds good."

Chapter Seven

"I'm not sure about this." Caroline eyed the four-man raft with what could only be foreboding.

"You're not scared, are you?" Gus grinned as he placed their lunches and extra clothes in the waterproof bags provided by the coordinators of the trip.

"Maybe a little. It's awfully small, don't you think?"

"It's standard size. You don't strike me as the type that scares easy." He straightened and stood, his hands on his hips as he eyed her anxiety attack.

"I don't. But I'm not familiar with rafting. What do I do besides hold on and not drown?"

Gus couldn't help it, he laughed and enveloped her in a hug. "I think that's the main part, delete the drowning. And I checked with the leaders when we got here; they're going to go over the fundamentals."

Caroline's hands rested at his waist and she leaned a bit into him. Gus resisted the urge to fold her in tighter, glancing over her head toward the other participants.

There were eight others in the party, ranging from college to middle-aged, buff to pudgy. A couple more women than men and every last one of them eyed the others with a range of emotions, from apprehension to excitement. But the question was, were the emotions directed toward the river trip or the possibility of getting hooked-up on the outing?

Caroline stirred in his arms and Gus reluctantly loosened his grip to allow her escape. She visibly squared her shoulders then approached their raft, as if facing down an enemy.

"Hi guys. Could you all gather round, up here, please?" One of the older women gestured toward the other boat and Gus held his hand out for Caroline to take. When she accepted it he tucked her to his side and joined the group. As they neared the others, he eyed the men who were scoping Caroline, sending out his signal. *She's mine, boys, back off.*

"For those of you new to the Sporty Singles' group, welcome. And for you older guys, no pun, help the newbies out with getting to know each other." The leader smiled widely, then continued.

The Single File 83

"I'm Willie, the president of the group and what that means is I'm the one who sets up stuff, so if you have an idea of something to do, let me know and I'll see what I can arrange. Now, for the trip today, we're rafting in a two raft party and the trip will cover about thirty miles of water, no more than level two water. If you've rafted before give me a show of hands." She paused while several people, Gus included, raised their hands. Caroline smiled up at him, and he hoped he remembered the lessons he'd learned in the rafting he'd done five years before.

Willie droned on, assigning raft positions, leaders, and emphasizing the use of floatation vests and whistles. A few minutes later Caroline was seated and Gus helped push off before joining her in the rear of the boat.

"Are you sure about the seats?" She sat completely straight, the tension evident in her posture and the fact that she didn't turn her head when she eyed their position.

"Relax. We're in the back, so we won't get too much lift when we go over the rocks and will get the benefit of the water."

"'Kay." She visibly swallowed as the raft picked up in speed.

He could tell she was still apprehensive but her mouth was set in stubborn lines, indicating her determination to see this through.

"Hey, do you like roller coasters?"

"Sure, who doesn't?" Her grip on the ropes fastened along the edges of the raft was so tight her knuckles were white.

"Well, this is a roller coaster on the water, only not as high."

"Oh, good. I'll get sick and wet at the same time. Hopefully I won't drown when I scream." She grimaced.

Gus laughed just as the leader, seated behind them, warned them of the upcoming rough water.

It was a wild ride, with plenty of white water to go around. As with the house project, Caroline's effort to row and carry her own weight impressed Gus. By the end of the trip, in spite of her face looking a little pale, Caroline also wore a wide grin. Gus climbed out of the raft in front of her then extended a hand. She took it and pulled herself out of the boat.

"That was so cool! I want to do it again." She vibrated with excitement and adrenaline.

Gus threw his head back and roared with laughter. "I told you it was like riding a roller coaster. You can't do it just once."

"Roller coasters have nothing on this. I'm going to do this again." Her smile dimmed a bit then she glanced toward the leaders, who were waiting for the transport vans at the edge of the clearing. "I need to do a little interviewing for the column."

Gus ran a hand along the cup of her shoulder, clad now in a wet shirt under her life vest. "Go ahead. I'll help belay the rafts and get them ready for loading."

She aimed for the coordinators and he joined the group of people emptying the rafts. A man near his age ambled up to him and grabbed a row. "She's a looker, huh."

Gus eyed him narrowly, "Pardon?"

"Blondie. Real cool though. Not stepping up to the job, you know?"

"You know, man, this is a situation I'd leave alone if I were you." Gus held on to his temper with effort.

"I'm just saying—"

"Don't." Gus straightened from pulling the raft from the water and glared at the other guy.

"Fine, didn't know you had staked a claim."

As the man stalked off Gus returned to his task. One thing the jerk was right about, though. Gus had staked his claim.

Caro finished her short interview with Willie and the other leader and turned to help pack up the supplies. As she approached her raft, she casually spoke to the other participants, getting their take on the journey. With the exception of one person, a motion sickness case, everyone thoroughly enjoyed the experience. She stacked several life vests and started toward the clearing. On her way, she glanced toward

Gus. He was deep in discussion of one of the more heavy-duty rapids with another rider, laughter evident in his eyes as he talked. At the end of the conversation, he turned toward her.

In an instant, Caro found herself caught up in his gaze. Warm, accepting and admiring. And it couldn't be her outfit or makeup. She was drying off from the drenching they got from the ride, but she knew her hair was still plastered to her skull and her shorts and heavy t shirt were damp and stained with dirt. Any makeup she'd worn that morning now resided under her eyes or had been washed away. Yet, in his eyes, she was attractive, and for the first time, she felt truly pretty, inside and out.

The vans arrived to transport them back to the car park and after helping Gus and others secure the raft to the top of one van, Caro scrambled into a seat. Gus followed her and stretched an arm behind her along the bench seat back. He grinned down at her, his eyes shining. "Do you have to go back to the office today or do you want to grab a bite to eat?"

"Are you kidding? After all the exercise we've done today, I deserve a burger. With fries. And cheese. And—"

"I got it," He laughed. "The works. And I know just the place."

"I'm sure of it." She grinned back at him and settled in for the ride back to the car and a chance to get to know this amazing guy more.

When she got home Caro had a voice mail. "Hi, Caroline. This is Miriah Lange. I've got some information for you regarding the matchmaking. I look forward to hearing from you."

Oh, great. Caro dialed Miriah. "Hey, what have you got?"

"Male, thirty-three years old, an accountant with a mortgage company here in Atlanta." Miriah rattled off, bringing to mind a police rap sheet.

"Okay. Now what?"

"I set up a date for you two to meet and you take it from there."

"Sounds simple."

"It is," Miriah sounded way too cheerful, proof positive it wouldn't be clear-cut at all.

"So how'd she do on the rafting trip?" Travis took a healthy drink of coffee.

Gus tilted his own mug and leaned into his recliner. "She did great. Wants to go again."

"You're kidding. I'd never place her as a rafting kind of girl. No makeup, no runways."

Gus swiveled his neck toward Travis. "I thought you liked her."

"I do, I just don't see it."

"She rode like a pro, held her own in the rowing—"

Travis laughed and waved a hand. "I give up, you're a goner."

"Huh?"

"Man, when a guy starts defending a woman to his best friend, he's officially gone over the edge."

Gus started to counter his friend's statement, but decided it wasn't worth the effort. Besides, he was right. He *was* over the edge over Caroline and he might as well admit it to himself.

"Don't laugh, bud. You're just as much at risk for falling for a lady as I am." Gus stood and headed toward the kitchen for more coffee. "Maybe more so. You've always been the one they flocked to."

He plucked the carafe from the coffee maker and turned, surprised to find his friend headed toward the door.

"Where you going? I thought we were going to find a game on the TV." Damn, he'd forgotten Travis hadn't dated since his accident.

"I've got to get going."

"Hey, was it something I said?" Gus followed his buddy.

"No. I'm just tired. Got to get up and get onto the transmission of the Grand Am tomorrow."

"You okay to drive?" Experience told Gus pushing Travis wouldn't get him anywhere. Besides, they'd never been able to talk things through much anyway.

"Yeah, I got the van's adaptations adjusted the other day. I can reach the pedals and everything." The bitterness Travis held at bay for years surfaced in a big way. "I'll see you tomorrow, all right?"

"Yeah, sure." Gus watched as Travis labored to roll his chair down the ramp of the house, to his adapted van and then heft himself into the vehicle. After four years, his upper body was heavy with muscle.

"Well, hell." He'd shoved his foot into his mouth once again.

Caro arrived at the restaurant a few minutes early and sat in the parking lot, then pulled out her cell phone. She dialed and waited anxiously for the answer.

"Hey. It's me. I'm here." She glanced around the parking lot, wondering if the man walking toward the restaurant was the one.

"Are you inside yet? Is he there? What's he look like?" Laney rattled off the questions in classic reporter fashion.

Caro chuckled, "I'm still in the car. I wish I had a shadow for the column tonight, like you did last year."

"It had its cons too, you know. I had Grant breathing down my neck watching all my mistakes."

"But you also had another pair of eyes." Caro took a bracing breath. "Look, I've got to go."

"Call me when the date with Mr. Maybe is over."

"Gotcha." Caro flipped her phone shut and her visor down to eye herself in the mirror. Makeup in place, not too heavy. Her eyes sparkled, though not with excitement. She refreshed her lipstick then headed toward the restaurant's entrance.

Inside, there was the typical dinner crowd, families with kids, couples and friends out for a relaxing evening. She gave her name to the hostess and was surprised when she was directed to a table near the windows. Seated with his back to her was a tall, muscular man with dark brown, almost black hair. She followed the hostess to the table and stopped at her chair and faced her date.

"Hi, I'm Caroline."

He stood, over six feet easy and held his hand out. "Hi Caroline, I'm Nick." He gestured for her to sit. So he got points for standing when she entered, but had the same deleted when he ended up sitting before she did. It felt a little like a job interview.

But, holy moley, he was handsome. Movie star handsome. Tall, dark and— well, handsome, handsome. Miriah's talent quotient increased in that instant.

"What do you want to drink?" He didn't glance at the menu featuring frilly drinks, nor did he yammer about the quality of the drinks. He ordered and then arched a brow toward her.

"I'll have an iced tea, unsweetened." She thanked the drinks waiter and focused her attention on Nick, determined to make the most of the date, though he wasn't the guy she wanted to be with right now.

"So, Miriah mentioned you're an accoutant?"

"That's what I put on the application."

Caro frowned, "It isn't what you do for a living?"

"Nah. I have to put something like that on the applications 'cause most places like that little joint won't accept me if I tell what I really do."

"And that is—"

"Cards." He sipped his drink as his gaze traveled up and down her. "You're very pretty, you know."

"Thank you. Cards?"

"Yeah, I play cards for a living. You know, poker. I've been in Mississippi for a while, Vegas before that."

Caro quelled a shudder of distaste. Great. Still, she had to at least make an effort to finish the evening. "And do you do well, at cards?"

His smile totally smeared his good looks all to heck. She'd never seen sinister before, but this looked like a pretty good imitation.

"I do good. Real good. And you look real good." He grinned at her. "What do you do, honey?"

"I work with the state police. Detective."

His grin disappeared and he immediately started

scoping the room. "Yeah? I thought that chick said—"

Chick? Caro ploughed ahead. "Yes. I work in Vice. So, Nick, what brings you to Atlanta, and are you staying long?" She finished with a drawl, her middle Georgia accent lengthening exponentially with his glare. This was fun!

"I'm on vacation. Just a few days, you know?"

Caro hummed, let him take that as he would. "It might be a good idea, leaving in a few days."

"You're a looker. Like a movie star. We'd make a good looking couple." His gaze returned to her and Caro decided her stomach couldn't take more.

She smiled thinly. "I don't think so. I'd hate to date you then have to arrest you."

He shot back the rest of his drink before answering her. "You may look good but you're not much to talk to, are you?"

She ignored her drink and stood, her purse securely tucked at her side. "Thank you for the drink, Nick. Have a safe trip back to Mississippi."

She walked out of the family restaurant, sure and not too quickly, though she wanted to jog. Outside, she dialed Laney.

"Why are you calling now? It's only been half an hour—" Laney began.

"Don't tell me some of your dates weren't as successful." Caro plucked her car keys from the pocket of her purse and unlocked her car.

Laney's chuckle soothed her hurt feelings. "So, it was a winner, huh? Was he unable to carry on a conversation? In awe of your beauty? What?"

"He was gorgeous, straight out of Hollywood. He talked." Maybe too much.

"So? What was wrong with him?"

Caro pulled out of the parking lot and headed toward the road. She'd drive a few miles, make a few extra turns and then head home, maybe with some Baskin Robbins and cookies, to boot.

She juggled her headset on and continued, "Well, you know how much I hate liars?"

"Yeah. Only you could have dates with guys that pretend to be doctors to influence you."

"Well, this guy's a professional card player."

"Wonderful. A professional liar." Laney chuckled.

"You got it. Not only did he lie on his application with Miriah but he lies for a living. But I didn't do every well." As good as she'd felt during the episode, she felt slightly smudged now.

"What'd you do, throw his drink in his face?"

"Nope, I lied."

She didn't hear anything. For a moment, she thought the line had been disconnected. Then, she heard breathing.

"You lied? You, who won't fib about your weight?"

"I lied, Laney. I can't believe I did it."

"But you did it for a good reason."

"To get out of the date?" Caro scoffed as she turned off the interstate at the Baskin Robbins' exit nearest the restaurant. Maybe she'd get a cone to go and some to take home. "You and I both know that I can be as snotty as a socialite when I want to. I could have gotten out of the date that way, if I wanted to."

"So what did you lie about?"

"I told him I was a Vice detective with the State Police."

Laney barked a laugh. "I love it."

"And it worked like a dream. He only came on to me once after that."

"Good for you. In that case, I think it was justified. Are you stopping by?"

"Yeah. Chocolate chip or pralines and cream?"

"Ah, go ahead and get a pint of each."

"My idea, exactly."

Gus wandered around the house for the better part of the day before giving up and heading out to the garage and workshed behind it. He found the chainsaw and attacked a fallen tree on the edge of the woods. He didn't need firewood in late April, but he'd stack it and have it come winter.

His body functioned like a well oiled machine, the

task almost automatic from years of practice. His mind divided between the wood chipping away into sawdust and neat lengths and the day he'd spent.

His long friendship with Travis assured they would get through any bump in the road. His mistake in talking about a lady for his friend would be forgiven, if not forgotten, without comment. He just needed his butt kicked for his big mouth. Since the accident Travis hadn't dated beyond the odd fixup by well meaning friends and family. So far, Gus had steered clear of that trap.

And Caroline. She had the job he hated above all. Her colleagues spent hours rummaging through garbage, real and figurative, to bring down people, both good and bad.

Did he trust her enough to open up to her? So far, he needed to be with her more than play it safe. But, would it be the safest thing for him, in the long run?

He finished the wood and stacked it near the edge of the wood pile then went inside to wash up. Afterwards, he rummaged through the fridge, in search of something to eat. Nothing lured him but the telephone.

A moment later, he gave into the urge and dialed Caroline's number.

"Hello."

"Hey, it's Gus."

"Gus, hi." She sounded inviting.

"What are you doing this evening?"

A pause, followed by her short laugh and, "You know, a woman isn't supposed to admit to not having a date on a weekend night. Especially the same night a man asks her out."

He grinned. She could have a date whenever. That she didn't have one meant she was particular in her choices. "So, are you going to admit it?"

"Yes. And I'd love to go out with you tonight."

"Great. I'll be over in half an hour." Just enough time to shower and change.

She laughed again. "Hold on a minute. I need a little more time than that."

"How much?"

"How about an hour?"

"Great. I'll see you then."

He hung up the phone, energized. An hour would give him enough time to plan.

Caro opened the door to Gus's knock, her smile widening at the sight before her. He stood, or rather leaned, against the door jamb. The small colorful bouquet of tulips should look odd in his large hand, instead they complimented his rugged handsomeness.

She retreated to let him enter and accepted the flowers. "Thank you. How'd you know I like tulips?"

"You aren't the roses type. Too predictable." He rumbled and let his gaze wander over her figure in appreciation.

"I'm unpredictable? That sounds dangerous."

"I'm sure you are, when you get threatened." He surveyed her apartment and Caro wondered what he really thought of her. The sensation of inadequacy was new for her and a bit unwelcome. "Besides, it was a compliment. You aren't what I expected."

Caro headed toward her kitchen and a vase for the flowers. "Thanks, I think." She ran water into the vase and plopped the flowers into it before turning to him. "Okay, I'll bite. What did you expect?"

"I figured you'd want roses, candlelit dinners, that sort of thing."

"I do, sometimes."

"But you're okay with barbeque, jeans and hammering on a house for someone else." He smiled at her and she suddenly felt giddy, almost dizzy.

"I like your place." He strolled to her bookcase and eyed its contents. A few volumes rested on the coffee table, along with others stacked willy nilly on the end tables.

"Thanks, it's a little messy, but it's mine. Now, where are we going and more importantly, am I dressed okay?"

His gaze flowed over her before he answered, "Jeans and a sweater are fine." He rubbed his hands together and grinned boyishly. "Now, you ready?"

Caro grabbed her purse and led the way to the door, "Is it okay if I ask for what?"

"You'll see."

"Another surprise. Oh boy."

"Another?" He rested his hand at her waist as they approached his truck.

"You. You're the first surprise."

"I can't believe I'm doing this." She wiped a bead of sweat from her forehead and braced herself.

"You don't like softball?" Gus looked at the bats offered and chose one for her.

"I love it, but usually I'm in the stands, not on the field." She accepted the bat and shouldered it, trying to remember the picture she had in her mind from the games she'd seen and the few intramurals she participated in.

Travis wheeled up to them. "You guys going to get a lineup or what?"

"We're ready. Caroline's going first, then me and Frank last. You ready for a whupping?" Gus grinned then winked at Caro.

"Ha. I've got Merry and George. Okay, let's get going." Travis wheeled around and sped toward the pitcher's mound.

"He's something, isn't he?" Caro marveled at the speed and power of Travis's arm as he threw some practice pitches to his catcher, a lean older woman with a gray braid down her back.

The Single File 99

"He was all-state in college." Gus eyed her with another grin. "You ready?"

"As I'll ever be."

"Okay. Since this is a pickup game, we're short on men. If you hit the ball, you run as fast as you can. The catcher is covering home and third, and George is covering first and second. Don't try to steal, Travis has eyes in the back of his head."

"Don't worry. My mother taught me never to steal." She quipped. Any successful hit, if her bat connected with anything, was unlikely to go anywhere.

She approached home plate and crouched, the bat at her shoulder. Travis grinned then tossed her a soft one. She swung, spun around and ended up facing Gus. Strike one.

He grinned at her encouragingly, "Try again."

She nodded, determined to succeed this time. She tried to remember her intramural softball days. It had to be the same, right? Flex the knees, elbows out, bend a little at the waist. Or was that golf?

She saw the pitch coming in time to jump back. Strike two. "Sorry about that. You okay?" Travis glanced toward Gus, who'd come to her side immediately.

Caro waved her date away and reassured Travis. "I'm fine. Throw another one."

She leaned into the swing this time and felt the

impact of the bat against the ball. For an instant she stood still, not really believing it. Then, aware of the yells behind her, she took off, running toward a base. Faster and faster she ran, approaching the plate. Suddenly, she got—tackled?

She hit the dirt, skidded along and came to a stop just a hand's length away from the prize. She stood, her hands braced on her hips, ready to face down the jerk who kept her from her goal.

Gus stood inches from her, his expression bouncing from exasperated to concerned, with a little smile playing around the edges of his mouth. "You okay?" He put a hand on her shoulder.

"What'd you do that for? I was almost to the base!" She brushed his hand away and patted at her jeans and T-shirt, dusting the grass and dirt off.

"I want to win." He shrugged and replaced his hand on her shoulder, steering her back toward the home plate.

"I do too. So, why'd you stop me?"

"Because you were headed toward third base." He waved a hand toward his team mates lined up, ready to bat. "Go ahead, Frank. I'll bat last."

"I ran for third?" She sat on the bench, already getting stiff from the inadvertent slide.

"Yep."

She could feel her face heat as the realization kicked in. When she could speak around the huge knot of humiliation in her throat, she muttered, "I guess that's why the team captain put me in left field in college. I guess I just got too excited and didn't pay attention."

Gus chuckled, "Sorry I tackled you. But the rules are, if the opposing team goes the wrong way, we get the point."

"Stupid rule. Who made that up?"

He leaned forward, his elbows on his knees and faced the ball field then turned to grin at her. "I did. Besides, I like tackling you."

She sputtered a moment before giggling, then laughing aloud. "I have a confession to make."

"What's that?"

"You know the intramurals I played in college?"

"Yeah."

"Well, I only played in one game and a couple of practices. My part-time job interfered too much. I'm not much of a ball player."

"I don't know. You do a pretty good job knocking things out of the park."

The game went along at a snail's pace. Caro struck out a few more time, her confidence shaken. Gus good heartedly urged her on, as did their team mates. In the end, though, they lost to Travis's team, big time.

They had footlong hot dogs at a local drive in restaurant, then went back to her apartment.

Inside, she made coffee. "I don't have dessert. Other than ice cream, if you like."

"Coffee's fine." He lounged on the sofa, his arms spread along the back. She poured two cups of coffee and brought them to the couch. Remembering his preferences, she served his drink black and then added milk to her own. She sank onto the sofa beside him and stretched out her legs with a sigh. Gus's hand brushed her shoulder, sending a small shiver through her.

"Are you sore?" His eyes gleamed over the edge of his mug as he sipped his coffee.

"Just a little stiff. It just occurred to me that the majority of time I'm spending with you I end up with bruises and sore muscles."

"Not my fault, or at least none of them other than this one."

"I guess I'm not used to doing activities this physical."

"I imagine you were on the sorority intramural teams, cheering the frat boys in college, huh."

She pointed her finger at him, "Ha. There you are. I didn't belong to a sorority. The one time I played in an intramural game I played for my dorm."

He playfully grabbed her finger and bit the tip. "So, you want to try another game next week?"

"Maybe, but give me some time to brush up on the rules, first." She gently pulled her finger away, too shaken by the attraction she felt for him and leaned forward for her coffee. She sipped it in an effort to find some thing to do with her hands, her eyes.

His hands fiddled with her hair, the light brush of his fingers against her neck offsetting the warm comfort of the coffee. She had to find a way out of the tension, before she did something foolish.

"I want a choice this time."

"A choice?"

"Um hmm. I get to choose what we do on our next date."

"And we're going out on another date?" His smile, sure and steady, warmed her inside and out, as she felt her cheeks heat in a blush.

"I—" She wasn't sure what she'd have said had he not leaned forward and kissed her. He enfolded her in his arms, warm and flush against his chest. The kiss lasted minutes, or hours. She wasn't sure.

When they surfaced, Gus tucked a strand of hair behind her ear. "For the record, we *are* going out again. And you get to choose, this time."

"I need to go on another assignment for the singles' column. Will you go with me?" Her mind muddled from the kiss, she scrambled to remember what her assignment was this time.

"Sure. What are we building this time?"

"Words. We're going to a Scrabble Party."

Chapter Eight

"Undulate." The elderly man crowed at his word and quickly added the points as Gus leaned back and surveyed Caroline. As partners in the game, they were seated opposite each other and couldn't really communicate without an audience. Not exactly what he'd pictured when he agreed to the outing.

She really outshined every other woman in the room. Not only was she beautiful but she charmed every man, old and young, brilliant and dense. And there really were some thick skulls in the room. In the course of the evening, words such as "neer," "exactamundo" and "fremmed" had been attempted, and not to gain points.

Gus played "off" as his word without thought. "Oh, Gus, you aren't going to win any prizes with

The Single File

that word, my friend." Phyllis, the woman to his left leaned forward, showing off her assets, if not her letters, and patted his arm. Gus heard the growl from across the table and arched a brow at Caroline. She smiled sweetly at him and plunked her word down.

" 'Showoff.' That's eleven points." Caroline leaned back in her chair and glared at Phyllis, who obviously didn't get the message, but Gus did.

The game continued for another twenty minutes before Harry won and a break was called. The whole room stood, stretched and wandered over to the refreshment table. Gus commandeered a couple of sodas and served Caroline before herding her over to chairs set off in the corner of the community room.

"I really need to talk to the hostess, Gus." She sipped her drink and glanced around the room, searching for the coordinator of the event.

"Give me five minutes."

"Okay, five. What do you think of the game?"

Gus leaned forward, his elbows resting on his knees. "Caroline, I wasn't really looking to get interviewed about the evening."

"Sorry." She fidgeted with her drink cup, peeling at the edges of the cardboard cup.

"Are you nervous?" It wasn't their first date, by any means, yet she acted as if it were.

"No, all right, yes. I guess I am."

"Why?"

She shrugged, "Not sure. I guess we're at that stage."

"What stage?" Even blushing and uncomfortable, she was appealing, maybe even more so than when she was in control of everything.

"The stage where we have to decide if we're going to go on to the next level in dating. You know, dating exclusively, declaring a relationship, that sort of thing. Oh, God, I'm babbling."

"Maybe a little. I'm curious. There are stages in dating?" This was news to him.

"Of course there is. The first date is just that, an initial opportunity to make a first impression, decide if you have anything in common, see if there is any attraction, that sort of thing."

"Got it." He nodded in encouragement.

"Then by the second date, you have to decide if the first time was an aberration or if the attraction is on target. Also, you get the chance to recover from the first-time jitters."

She obviously believed everything she said, and it sounded good so far. Besides, it gave him more insight into what made Caroline tick.

"By the time the third to fifth date comes around, it's crunch time. Kisses, hugs, close physical contact happens around this time, if not before. And that's when you either—"

"Fish or cut bait," he finished.

She grimaced, "I'd pick another analogy, but yes. It's the time you decide if the other person is worth risking a relationship."

"For the record, you're worth the risk." He wanted to kiss her but it wasn't the place or time, with their audience.

Her smile lightened the room, it was so bright. "I think so too, you."

"You want to stay for the rest of the evening or get out of here?" The thought of playing yet another unending round of wordplay without her within touching distance was his idea of torture.

"I have to interview some people. If I can do that in the next fifteen minutes or so, you've got a deal." She patted his forearm then stood and advanced into the knot of people near the refreshments.

Content to sit out of the fray, Gus watched her as she mingled and chatted. In the space of ten minutes, she managed to talk to everyone in the room, covering around twenty people, then separated a middle-aged woman from the pack. Her skills as in investigator were clearly wasted in her society column.

By the end of her fifteen minute limit, she'd gotten her interview and was free to spend more time with him. He gathered her sweater and draped it over her shoulders. Then he clasped her shoulder and drew her close as they left.

"What do you say we go sightseeing?" They headed toward the truck.

"It's nine o'clock at night." She grinned and leaned into him.

"Just what we need." He opened the door then bracketed her small waist with his hands and lifted her into the truck.

She accepted his comment without any other reference to it. Instead they talked about the game night and singles they'd met in the event. Gus maneuvered the truck through the streets of Atlanta and left the city rapidly, the evening traffic thinning as he left town.

They left the lighted streets and approached the country lanes of rural Georgia. Caroline glanced around, intrigued. "I didn't realize there was as much country still around the city."

"There is if you know where to look. Are you a country mouse or city mouse?"

"City. I grew up in Nashville. When I graduated college I moved here. Obviously I haven't gotten around enough."

"Yeah, well if you've been traveling because of your job, you wouldn't have a lot of social events in this neck of the woods. Nashville, huh?"

"Yes. And no, I didn't sing country music, just listened, like every other teenager. Nashville's more cosmopolitan than you'd think. It's more than cowboy hats, guitars, and sequins."

"I've been there a couple of times, for work. I liked it."

Caro glanced outside the window of the truck. The trees were mature, full of spring leaves. Fragrant spring flowers and grasses filled the air, along with the fresh dirt smell from a nearby creek or spring.

"Can we walk or is this private land?"

"It's private, but we can get out. And star gaze, if you like." Gus pulled off the main road and onto a small, private lane.

"Are you sure?"

"I'm positive. It's my land."

Wow. In this area, even out of the main city, land like this sold for a premium. How did a guy who owned a garage afford something like this?

"How much land is there?"

"Around fifteen acres. I have three landscaped around the house. The rest, I've left the way I got it, other than to check for falldowns every so often."

"Falldowns?" She turned from eyeing the surroundings outside the truck to glance at him.

"Trees that have been blown down by wind or disease, things like that. I clear them out to keep the land navigable."

"It must be nice, to be able to get away."

"It is." Gus pulled into a gravel parking space near a cedar covered house. Caro suppressed the urge to ask for a tour and instead followed him up steps and around the deck.

"I have a couple of telescopes set up for clear nights like this. It kind of puts things into perspective."

"Why do you need to do that?" She waited while he stationed the telescopes then stepped up to one and peered into it.

"Doesn't everyone need to, every now and then? Life gets too cluttered, too busy. Looking at the sky puts things in order for me."

He stepped up behind her and reaching around, twirled some dials on the telescope. "See anything?"

"Yes. What is it?" An array of stars shone before her, bright and sparkling.

"Do you see the red one, kind of to the left and up from the center?" At her murmured assent, he continued, "That's Mars."

She looked and listened to his low voice as he described constellations and stars, planets and more. As they watched the world around them, she felt the ground melt away, along with her anxieties about dating him. Gradually, everything made sense, Gus and his friend Travis, dating him, and a possible future.

As time passed, small clouds scuttled into view and finally covered the sky. A slight wind blew up, sending shivers down Caro's arms. Even covered with her sweater, she felt the spring chill.

Gus ran his hands up and down her arms, warming her. "I'd better get you home before you get too cold."

"Thanks." She glanced up toward the sky one last time before she turned away. "I never realized how peaceful it is."

He smiled and held out his hand. Caro accepted it and walked with him to the truck.

"It's even better when you share it with someone." He opened the door and helped her into the truck. "What are we doing tomorrow?"

"Tomorrow?" She didn't bother to tamp down the happiness this time.

"Yeah. Want to spend some time together?"

"I do."

"So, we'll do something. What do you want to do?"

She shrugged. "I don't care. Just spend time with you."

He leaned in and gently kissed her before closing the door and rounding the truck.

Well, that did it. She'd declared it. Her wish to go forward.

The next afternoon, Gus made an effort to concentrate on his work instead of on Caroline. She sat, or rather perched on a metal stool, her eyes constantly surveying the world around her. At the base of the stool lay Haggis and Buford, intent and adoring.

"How long does it take to rebuild a car like this?" She gestured toward the Grand Am.

Travis divided his attention between the transmission he cleaned and her question. "Depends on the car. Gus got a good deal on this one, but it's going to take a while. He grinned toward Gus and Caroline, the observant reporter she was, caught the intent behind it.

"Good deal? What good deal?" She left her station and leaned down to pet Haggis as she directed the question toward Gus.

"I found it in a junkyard."

"A—"

"Told you he got a great deal. Fifty bucks for the whole thing." Travis chuckled and wheeled into the back room to retrieve more cleaning fluid.

Gus straightened from the engine and wiped his hands on a rag. "I found the car when I was looking for spare parts for a customer. It was in lousy condition but there was something about it. I basically paid enough to get it out of the scramble it was in and towed it in."

"So, how much work will it take to get it in running condition?" She approached the car and glanced inside before looking toward him.

"Another month or so, a few dollars and some TLC. Then it'll be in prime condition."

"That's a lot of work to get a car going." She approached him, her slim hand gliding along the car's side panel as she walked.

"Everything worth having is worth working for." He met her half way along the car and then leaned his hip against the car, facing her.

She mirrored his position and tilted her head up to meet his gaze. "Everything?"

"Yeah, especially the important things in life." He leaned down and brushed his lips along hers, then firmed the kiss as she leaned into it. In the distance he heard the radio chattering away and Travis' voice. He started to gather Caroline into his arms when a sharp jab to his ribs made him withdraw.

"Sorry to interrupt but you need to take this." Travis gave him an apologetic smile and extended the garage's cordless phone.

Gus cleared his throat and smoothed his hand down Caroline's shoulder as he put the phone to his ear. "Yeah?"

In the last few years, Gus found himself staying in the office later and later, seven days a week, or on the road between properties. Until Caroline.

"Sorry boss, but we need you here." Lately, David Hubbard, as vice president, picked up more of the daily grind. Gus had dealt with acquisitions and basic principles.

"Why?"

"The South Carolina contract may have some flaws. Legal wants to go over it with you."

"Now?" When he wanted, needed, to spend more time with Caroline?

"Now. Unless you want the property to slip through."

Gus sighed, "No. I'll be down in half an hour. Tell Legal to draft some alternatives for the problem clauses."

He disconnected the call and tossed the phone to Travis. Caroline eyed him, her curiosity evident.

"I've got to deal with something for a couple of hours. Can I call you later?" He tucked a strand of hair behind her ear.

"Sure. I can go into the office and type up my columns for this week."

What was he doing with a lawyer? Caro maneuvered her car through the late afternoon traffic toward the newspaper office. As a reporter she had an insatiable curiosity. Normally, she'd investigate but now she couldn't do that. Or could she—

No! No, no, no. You're past that.

She swerved into the turn lane and made a quick left into the parking lot of the Globe. Great, Laney's car was in its usual place beside Grant's sporty Corvette. Gus'd like that one, she mused. Maybe she'd ask Laney and Grant to dinner with Gus. "Help. I'm thinking in couples, now," she scolded herself.

She jogged into the building, intent on finding Laney and putting two minds to the problems she had.

Laney tapped away on a column, her attention focused on the activity. Caro entered Laney's work area and shifted a stack of paper before sliding into the chair beside Laney and staring her down.

"Hold on, hold on." Laney hammered away.

Caro tapped her foot in exasperation while her friend completed and saved her work. Laney pushed away from the desk and stretched, turning her easy smile toward Caro. It disappeared as soon as she took Caro's anxiety in and she leaned forward.

"What's wrong?"

"I'm in trouble."

"How? Something with your mom? The paper? What?"

"Gus."

Laney rose from her seat. "I'll kill him, what's he done?"

"Nothing. He's great. I'm so busted." She'd never been this afraid in her life, nor as excited.

Laney stared at her for a minute before breaking into a wide grin. She shot her hands into the air, more indicative of a teenager after a score in a ball game than a mature newspaper reporter.

"You've done it, haven't you?" She pointed a finger at Caro. "You've fallen for him."

Caro folded her body, resting her head on her knees, suddenly overwhelmed. She mumbled, "In all the years I've dated, it's never been like this."

Laney patted her head. "I know, kiddo. Believe me, I know." She stood and grabbed Caro's hand then pulled. "Let's get out of here. This isn't private enough to talk."

They strode toward the elevator. As they neared the far end of the room, the business editor sauntered into the aisle. Caro slowed then stopped a few feet away, anxious to get away from curious eyes and busy minds, yet reluctant to let anything slip.

"Franklin, what's new in the market?"

"Some things up, others down. What are you doing leaving?"

Laney stepped up, to blast Franklin, Caro was sure, but she stalled the movement by sliding in front of Laney. This she could handle.

"I'm sorry, Frank. Did you need some help with your department? I'm sure I can find the time between the columns I'm writing."

The usual buzz in the newsroom dampened near them; clearly her voice carried as the other worker bees hushed to listen in. Maybe this would be in the next column of Home Life.

A flush blotched his face, mimicking a bad sunburn. "Look, lady, just because you go to soirées and out with set up dates and write your little essays—"

"And still find time to do research, which I'm gearing up to do right now. Now, if you'll excuse me—" She arched an eyebrow at him when he hesitated.

Laney nudged Caro a couple of inches to the right and peered over her shoulder, "You moving or what, Frank?"

"Franklin," he hissed and shifted aside. Caro and Laney walked on, silent, but the room behind them erupted in whispers and quiet laughter, with an odd hoot chiming in.

They rode down the elevator with some chuckles, recounting the expression on Franklin's face when he slumped back to his desk.

"I know he's been after you to date him for a while, but what does old prune face have against you?" Laney crossed her arms and stared at the indicator light.

Caro shrugged, "The fact that I went out with him and didn't want to do it again, I guess."

"With coworkers like that—"

"Don't share an inkwell, I know." A poisoned pen, or its equivalent, seemed to be in her future, but Caro was proud of her stand against Franklin.

The elevator neared the bottom floor and Laney stepped forward, "Well, the bum totally blew my mood."

Caro laughed and led the way to the building's exit. "I bet a caramel chocolate latte will put it back to order."

"Only if it has whipped cream."

The time it took to order and receive the caffeine and sugar laden drinks gave Caro another chance to recognize the butterflies fluttering in her stomach.

They found a corner table and settled with their coffees. Laney sipped hers and sighed, "That's better. Now, back to serious business. Tell me about Gus."

"He's the genuine thing, Laney. Straight forward, a good friend to his buddies, hard working—And the dates we've gone on are perfect."

"Romantic and candlelit?" Laney grinned.

"No. Funny, outrageous, messy," Caro shrugged, "You know the dates we've had. I've hammered nails, been covered in drywall dust, and been more sweaty than any other time of my life. And wet? I rode white water in a raft! And didn't care that my hair was in my eyes and dripping wet. And I went stargazing—" She halted when she met her friend's understanding gaze.

"It's about time. I've seen you date guys that see your surface, not the real you. No one would think to take you to a barbeque place that looks more like a hole in the wall. Any guy that's willing to do that, to take you to the real world and not what he thinks a woman like you would like, is okay in my eyes."

Caro shifted her gaze to her drink, the whipped cream melting and merging with the darker coffee under it. "It's scary, though. What if he doesn't reciprocate?"

"What do the signs tell you?"

Caro smiled at the memory of Gus's kisses, his gentle touches. Laney returned her smile and lifted her mug in a toast. "Enough said."

"I'm taking a big risk you know."

"But think of the payoff."

They chatted a few more minutes before Laney turned her focus back to Gus. "I thought you were spending the day out of the office, doing stuff with Gus and getting ready for the Spring Gala."

"I was. I did my pre-gala interviews this morning and went into the garage to see Gus and Travis, but he had something come up and had to leave."

"Sorry about that. I hate when Grant has to go out of town. He's gone to Charlotte to cover the column there for a few days. Makes it lonely."

Caro nodded absently, going over the call Gus received before leaving the garage. "I wonder—"

"Yeah?"

"Well, Gus got a call before he had to leave. Said

something about meeting a lawyer. I wonder if he's having some financial trouble."

"He didn't seem to, did he?"

Caro sipped her coffee and gathered her thoughts. "I don't know. He owns a garage, along with his friend, Travis. But, you know, that's about all I do know about him."

Laney's brow furrowed as she processed. "He owns a garage and needs a lawyer. He could be incorporating."

"Why? He owns a single business. I don't know a lot about industry but a business would incorporate to protect interests or resolve some differences with people, right?"

Laney shrugged, indicating her equal ignorance of the business life and Caro continued, "Travis and Gus get along really well, from what I can see. The garage has a car in the bay and they seem pretty busy every day."

"But is there any indication he has money troubles?"

Caro shook her head, "Not that I can see. Although, the garage doesn't have business other than the car rebuilding, so it may not make a lot of money. It doesn't matter either way, I just hope he isn't having some difficulties."

"Well, honey, either you have to accept that he's got other business you don't know about or he's just writing his will."

Caro grimaced at the last comment, but the suggestion of "other business" got her thinking. What did she know about Gus, really?

Gus rubbed his eyes, trying to ease the ache from reading fine print and arguing the minutiae of the contract before him. God, this was why he needed carburetor rebuilds and his log splitting.

"Look, gentlemen. Either we come to a conclusion tonight, or the deal is null and void." He'd had it with all this crap.

The owner of the property shot a startled glance at him and rushed to assert his stand. "I only needed a clarification on the options' clause."

"Which we covered a couple of hours ago. Then we talked about the environmental protection and safety measures that are standard and more than adequate for the business. Now, Mr. Wilson, let's get to the real purpose of the meeting. Have you had other offers for the land?" And how much was he upping the price?

A telltale shift of the eyes toward his companion told Gus more than the past five hours' of haggling. He pushed away from the desk and strode to the window of his office. In the background Hubbard continued the rumble with his steady nature.

Street lights muted the features of the night sky and the parking lot held only a few vehicles, including his truck. It seemed like old times when he had no life other than the business and the old garage. But no more, he had better things to do than get another ulcer.

He turned with a purpose. "Okay, here's what we'll do. We're going to call an end to the meeting and any further negotiations." He held a hand up to forestall any arguments, "The contract has to stand as it is, that's my final offer. If it's unacceptable to you, Mr. Wilson, then by all means, take another offer. I can find another piece of property for Hill's Garage Works. South Carolina is a big state."

He won the staring contest by starting to gather his jacket and cell phone. Hubbard hid a smile and ushered the suddenly reluctant men out with a calm, "Call us with your decisions, and have a safe trip back."

Hubbard closed the door with a bark of laughter. "Well, you may not get that piece of land, but you won the war, Gus."

"Yeah, I just wish I hadn't wasted the five hours we took to get to the ultimatum." He could have spent the hours in a much more productive manner, such as cleaning out a gas line or ash tray of his makeover. And spending time with Caroline.

"So, boss. We're clear on that issue. Do you want to go over the other properties tonight or later?"

Gus eyed Hubbard. "Don't you have a personal

life, Dave? You spend fourteen to sixteen hours a day here and you're asking for more?"

Dave shrugged, "I'm divorced, don't want another mistake of a relationship. And I like the job."

"So did I, but I needed something else to do, as well."

Dave grinned, "Travis mentioned you've found something else to focus on lately. Nice lady?"

"Very nice." And she meant more than any other woman had in a very long time. Maybe it was time to share the fact with the lady.

"Go home, Dave. That's what I intend to do." Gus pocketed his cell phone, grabbed his briefcase and led the way out of the office. Hubbard followed him, turning off lights as they walked. At the parking lot, they separated and Hubbard gave him a last salute. Gus glanced at the dashboard display, one thirty in the morning. No, he couldn't call her now. But tomorrow morning, he'd talk to her then. His headache eased as he thought of her and the prospect of seeing her again, soon.

Chapter Nine

Caro surveyed her closet, trying to find a dress she could wear to the Spring Gala. The annual event, sponsored by the Ladies Guild Society, usually drew the cream of Atlanta society, intent on securing their place in the social order of modern Georgia. Business deals, romance and marriage plans, as well as some of the less savory deals were haggled and closed during the event, and the press of Atlanta covered it from all angles.

In addition to the society columns of the major papers, business reporters and lifestyle columnists such as Caro, as well as fashion photographers and reporters clambered for invitations or camped out in the parking lot of the historic hotel, The Georgian Terrace.

Luckily, Caroline had secured an invite to the function, her first and a coup for the *Globe*. Now, to find a dress.

She sighed, "With my salary, I can't afford anything new and snazzy enough to impress. So, what now?"

Every formal dress in her closet had been worn at least a couple of times and to wear it now, at the most important event of the year for the society column, would be a mistake she'd regret. Such a minor detail could mean this gala could be her only one, or worse, other society events would be closed to her, or other society reporters from the *Globe*. Though she might not be as ambitious as Laney, Caro still prided herself in her efficiency.

Frustrated by her meager bank account and full but hopeless closet, she turned her attention to other aspects of her job.

She reviewed her last event, the Scrabble game party, and realized she hadn't found another possibility. The *Single Life* column continued to have good readership, partly because of the novel events and news she gave each column. Now, she was coming up empty.

A brief scan of her notes on special interest gatherings revealed singles groups that were too narrow for her tastes, even as an objective reporter. So, what could she do that could put another twist on the dating scene?

She rifled through her notes and set aside castoffs, until she came to a business card, neatly clipped to an e-mail. Miriah Lange. The matchmaker who didn't have a clue, she mused. Still, it was worth a shot to try again, and she had the feeling she'd have to prod Miriah a bit to get her to try again.

After a few rings, her call was answered by an out of breath Miriah.

When she mentioned another shot at the matchmaking attempt, Miriah reacted just as she'd expected. "You want to try again?" Miriah sounded as if it were torture, which wasn't too far from the truth with the card shark date Caro had endured.

"I felt like the match I had may have not covered the story well enough. Could we try again?" Caro urged.

"Well, I supposed I could—Give me a couple of days, all right?"

Caro's stomach dropped; her singles column needed to be turned in within a couple of days, which meant she needed information from Miriah. Well, if the matchmaking didn't come through, maybe she could interview Miriah.

"Do you think I could come by, maybe tomorrow morning?"

Miriah was silent then assented, "I guess so, but I won't have a name—"

"That's okay," Caro assured her. "We can talk

about the process, maybe cast a little light on the mystery."

Miriah laughed, "It might even help me figure it out. Obviously I fumbled the first try."

Caro grimaced. She figured she had been Miriah's guinea pig. The twenty minute date, uncomfortable and interminable, affirmed that it took more than physical attraction to make a connection with a guy. Still, she hated to offend Miriah. "I guess we all need practice."

They ended the conversation and Caro returned to her evening chores. She'd kept busy all day, writing, researching singles groups in other areas and specialty groups, and generally trying to keep her mind off Gus. Why hadn't he called?

"And why does he have to call me every day?" Great, now she was talking to the wall. Not even a pet to ramble to.

Her newfound emotions for Gus were frightening enough. Now the dependence her happiness had on him terrified her more than anything ever had before.

"I have to do something!" But what? Laney, in a fit of loneliness, had hopped a plane to Charlotte that morning. No social activities appealed to her, so she turned to her old standby. Running.

She changed into her old sweats and T-shirt, pinned her house key into her pants and clipped on a mini radio. A nice mile or so would take the edge off her panic, she hoped.

Thirty minutes later, she rounded the corner of her street and slowed from a jog to a walk, cooling down. Fatigued muscles and dehydration didn't go far in ridding her of Gus's face, or his touch.

She let herself in the apartment and headed for the shower. Another day almost over and she'd not been reduced to calling Gus.

As she passed the bar separating her tiny kitchen and living room she caught the blink of her message machine. Hopeful, she punched the button.

"Hey, Caroline. I wanted to catch you this morning but it's been crazy at work. Call me when you get home." His voice rumbled over the speaker.

She rushed through the shower, too gritty and sweaty to call before. After donning her pajamas she dialed his number, by heart, darn it, and settled on the sofa.

"Hill."

"It's Caroline."

"Caroline, hey. You had to work late?"

"No, just out for a run." She didn't have a problem with telling him her business, but it should be reciprocal. "You?"

"I had a b–bear of a day. Everything went screwy from the time my alarm *didn't* go off."

"Poor baby. I had a great day. Just realized I didn't

have another angle on the singles column and I don't have anything to wear to the biggest social event of the session."

He chuckled, "Yep, our lives are exciting, huh."

"Exhilarating. Did you resolve your problem yesterday or was that part of the lousy day?"

"Resolved? Not really, but I did get some things settled. Nothing really earth shattering."

Okay, so he didn't want to talk about business, so what now?

"Any stars out tonight?"

"Somewhere, maybe, but not here. Cloud cover is too heavy, I think. I didn't check it out."

"Why? Didn't you mention that it helped with stress? Sounds like you needed it tonight."

His voiced lowered, if that was possible. "I didn't have the necessary elements to enjoy it."

"Huh?"

"You."

She smiled, charmed by his obvious flirtation. "Sorry. I had a great time, you know."

"You sound surprised."

She laughed, her stomach giddy and full of the resident butterflies again. "I've been surprised every time we're together. I didn't think I'd enjoy construction work or watching you slog away in a garage with Bassets slobbering on my feet, either. But I did."

"Do you think you could enjoy something tomorrow?"

"Like what?"

"Like an old fashioned dinner and a movie."

"Only if it's not a horror film."

"No, just blood and guts. Oh, and popcorn and mints."

"Great, just what I need."

"So, is it a deal? Movie and dinner tomorrow?"

"Okay. What time?"

"I'll pick you up around six?"

"I'll be ready."

Miriah's house looked a lot different when Caro arrived the next morning. Bolts of cloth covered every seating surface in the living room, with the exception of the horsehair sofa where they sat.

"Sorry, I'm kind of in the middle of something," Miriah shifted and pulled a small cloth bag from the side of the couch.

"You mentioned you were a design major in college, right?" Caro eyed the young woman's outfit. The skirt was a simple peasant style, but the embellishment around the hem wasn't machine-made, they were hand sewn. Ditto on the blouse, inexpensive cloth but obviously painstaking work. "Do you make all your own clothes?"

Miriah smiled, her expression wry. "Yes, it's

cheaper than buying what I want. Besides, if I can market my own stuff by wearing it, I'm more likely to get a job."

"Good luck." Fashion design was a hard field to break into, harder than the competitive field of journalism. But Miriah looked like she had talent.

Caro grinned, an idea occurring to her. "What are you working on right now?" She pulled out her camera.

"Nothing in material. I'm sketching, brainstorming with fabrics."

"Out of ideas?"

Miriah shook her head, "Just daydreaming, really. It's debut time, so I was fiddling with that."

Debut, debutantes, formals. Maybe—"Could I see?"

"Sure. They're pretty rough." Miriah stood and walked to the dining room, then returned to the sofa with a large sketch pad. Caro accepted it, turned the pages slowly, absorbing the creativity of the sketches.

Each page revealed a slim silhouette, the face indistinct, but the form and dress clear. The first dress was a deb's, clean lines, modest with a hint of sex appeal.

She deliberately slowed her examination of the pages, then closed the sketch book and returned it to Miriah. "I have a favor to ask."

"Sure, let me get the file on you."

Caro halted Miriah before she could rise from the sofa. "No, not that. Well, we'll get to that later, but I wanted to buy a dress."

"A dress?"

"Yes. I have a big party to go to this Friday night, and I need a killer dress. That is, if you have time to design and make it."

She smiled as a sparkle lit Miriah's eyes, making her pretty in a way she'd never appeared before. This might work.

They conferred on the gala's dress code, formal and expensive, the last of which Caro couldn't afford. Her additional requirements, nothing that would outshine other attendees, but something great looking. And Miriah had ideas.

She filled another book with sketches she rejected for one reason or another. Caro tried to stop her, there were plenty of really good ideas on paper.

"No, we need something really spectacular, but classy. Like your looks. Cool and classy, like—" Miriah studied her then continued, "Has anyone ever told you you resemble Grace—"

"Kelly, I know." Caro grimaced.

"How's that a bad thing?"

"It's not, on its face, but when you hear it from the time you're out of puberty, it gets old."

Miriah flipped to a fresh page of her book and started to draw, her hand whipping across the white surface in broad strokes. "Well, this time, we're going to use it to your, or our advantage."

The movie Gus suggested actually turned out to be a play and Caro thoroughly enjoyed herself. The cast was full of talent and the play, funny and poignant at the same time, was a remake of a Broadway smash. She glanced over at Gus as he weaved through the traffic on the way to her apartment. "You picked that play?"

"I thought you'd like it," he shrugged.

"I did. No music, no dancing, just jokes and dialogue."

"And no shoot 'em up, either. You missed out on your blood and guts movie."

"Nah, don't miss it. But I did miss the mints." She giggled and settled into the seat of the truck. Oh, it felt good to be here, with him.

"What about tomorrow night?" He reached over and touched her hand as it rested on her purse in her lap.

"I can't, the gala's tomorrow night." She turned her palm into his and marveled at the way his large hand engulfed hers.

An idea occurred to her, and why it shouldn't have before stunned her. "Would you go with me?"

"To this gala?" His tone made it sound as if she'd asked him to the musical he so obviously detested.

"Um, hmm. I have to cover it for the paper, and

it's a formal event. The food's supposed to be really first rate, though. And you'll make a long evening seem a bit shorter," she urged.

"So, a tux?"

"A tux. Will you have enough time to rent one?"

"Yeah. What time?" His grasp on her hand tightened marginally.

"It starts at eight, but I have to be there to start covering it by seven. Is that possible, or will you have to work late?"

"I'll pick you up at six thirty, tux and all. Powder blue okay with you?"

She giggled and squeezed his hand in return.

Caro didn't have to think about her *Single Life* column that day. The giddy feeling welled over into words, and for once she didn't bother separating her personal and professional lives.

Meeting a nice guy is difficult in any circumstance. But when you've been stung a few too many times, the baggage dragging behind you becomes too much of a burden to bring into a relationship.

Then you meet *him*. You wonder, what's he hiding? Is there a family tucked away in the past? When you find out there isn't anything to hide, you pinch yourself to realize he's for real. I met *him*, and his name is Gus. And he's the real thing. I'll keep you updated.

Gus straightened his tie as he approached Caroline's door. He loathed black tie deals, but it seemed important to her, so he'd gone out on a limb. And a very fragile one it was, too. It could backfire on him, big time.

For years, he'd avoided these things. While lots of business agreements were made at society functions, even more gameplaying went on. And the attempts he'd made at that kind of life, short lived and disastrous, had taught him he was better off where he was.

"A glorified grease monkey with good luck," he muttered and pressed the doorbell.

"Coming." Caroline's voice drifted through the door, followed by its opening. Good God. She was gorgeous.

Nothing had prepared him for this, he thought. She wore a light blue satin dress, classic in lines but it managed to hug her figure and remain discreet and classic.

"Hi, just let me get my wrap and we'll be ready." While he tried to find his voice she turned and grabbed a triangle of material that matched the dress. He took it from her and draped it over her shoulders, letting his hands linger for a minute on her bare arms. "You look beautiful."

Her glance over her shoulder was a blend of flirtation and caution. Had she heard the compliments so much that she didn't believe them anymore? He squeezed her shoulders and continued, "You'll need this tonight. It's a little cool outside."

"Thanks," she smiled and led the way to the elevator. As they exited the building, Gus allowed himself another long look.

The dress was an off-the-shoulder number, had a fitted waist and then flowed down to the floor where matching shoes peeked through with each step.

"Powder blue. Sorry I didn't follow through with my original thought."

Caroline laughed and smoothed a hand down the skirt of the dress as they entered the parking lot. "Was it from prom?"

"A friend's wedding. Should have known it wouldn't last when his fiancé talked him into powder blue velvet and yellow."

She giggled, "I can picture you in it. But it's probably a good thing you didn't wear your tux. We might have taken all the glory from the Ladies' Guild."

He laughed with her at the mental image of the two of them decked out in blue, making a wide swath along the red carpet. "Definitely don't want to give them a shock."

She came to a halt and glanced around the parking lot. "Where's the truck?"

"I didn't bring it. Good thing, too. You'd never make that first step in that dress."

"I wasn't planning on it. You'd have had to help me."

He stalled a bit then grinned, "I thought too much that time. I'd have been better off with the truck after all." He gestured toward the car parked at the end of the lot, his hand at her waist to lead her.

The luxury sedan sparkled in the reflected street light. "This is it?"

"Yep. I figured you needed a chariot worthy of you, Cinderella."

"Thanks," She murmured, surprised. How did he afford this? And did it have something to do with his mysterious call a few days ago?

On the way to the Georgian, they talked about interests, the university football team's chances that fall, the weather and future dates he had planned. Caro enjoyed the patter but wondered at the tense set in Gus's shoulders. He'd seemed okay with the idea of the event and didn't act nervous at all. Was he still worried about the call?

"Gus, do you mind if I ask you a personal question?"

"Sure, honey." He patted her hand in encouragement.

"The other day, you got a phone call at the garage. I was wondering—"

She paused, unsure whether she should go on. For all the comfort and ease they experienced in their dates, this was the first time she'd broached anything personal.

"Go on," His voice rumbled through the car, still quiet but not as relaxed as before.

"I couldn't help but overhear, you mentioned a problem and an attorney." Her courage, usually at the forefront in times of stress, deserted her.

After a time of silence, he glanced toward her then spoke, "It's okay. You need to know if there's a problem about my garage? I'll make it easy for you. I had a question from an attorney about a piece of land I wanted to buy. I had to go to a meeting about that."

She studied him, searching his face in the shadowed car for an indication of his mood. His usually open face was shuttered now.

"I'm sorry, I shouldn't have butted in your personal business." She needed to make things better, if she could. Otherwise, the evening she'd so looked forward to would be a torture instead.

"No problem. Now, get ready, we're here."

She turned to look and indeed, they were at the Georgian. Cars were lined up for the valet parking and couples exited the vehicles in their finery. Caro turned her attention reluctantly toward her job and instructed Gus to turn into the area marked for the press.

He parked and escorted her to the edge of the throng of people dressed in an assortment of outfits, from jeans and T-shirts to formal wear much like theirs. Caro snagged her photographer and towed him along behind her, Gus bringing up the rear. She briefly instructed the photographer on the individuals and couples she wanted photos of, then at his look of panic, told him to photo anyone dressed in formal attire and she'd go over the shots later for identity. With that, he escaped and Caro blasted her editor for assigning her a novice on this important night.

Gus eyed the crowd as they approached the entrance. "Photos that important?"

"For this event they are. Everyone who's anyone begs for an invitation for this thing, and when they get the invite, move heaven and earth to get a photo in one of the papers. It can mean the difference between a debutante making her reputation, of a businessman getting the deal. Yes, it's important and English doesn't understand it."

"Who's English?" He cupped her elbow as they stepped up to be introduced.

"My editor for the society column. She's great in

the crime field, but hasn't any interest in the column I do. As long as it shows up in the paper and gets good reviews itself, she's satisfied."

They came to a stop at the entrance of the ballroom, near the top of the stairs. Caro's gaze swept the room, taking in the array of costumes.

Many of the women had opted for antebellum styles and their escorts had the same idea, dressed in military inspired formal attire.

Gus stood sentinel at her side, silent. She led the way to a refreshment table then glanced at him, "I need to do some mingling. Are you okay with it?"

"Sure, I'll get a drink and wait for you." He scanned the room, his eyes narrowed, then turned to her. "Or do you want me to go with you?"

She did but also realized how uncomfortable he was in the mix. "I'll be fine. I'll see you in a few minutes and then we can relax, okay?"

"Sure."

Gus spent the first thirty minutes or so of the evening hovering. Hovering on the periphery of the ballroom, hovering around the refreshment table, hovering at the edge of the dance floor. Then, when he noticed the throng of men clustered around Caroline, he decided to stop hovering. He approached her. The men surrounding her parted the way and he stepped to Caroline's side.

She tilted her head and smiled at him then finished

the question she had for Raymond White, the head of the largest bank in the city. Gus remained silent, his gaze on her as she deftly maneuvered the conversation through business and personal questions, gaining information that could garner a column all by itself. White glanced toward Gus and received a slight shake of his head. They'd met several times in the course of Gus's building his business and hopefully White would keep his mouth shut.

"Gentlemen, thank you for your time. Please thank your wives and dates for my interruption." When she stepped a bit closer to Gus he took the hint and took her elbow.

"Caroline, you've brightened the room tonight. If this guy doesn't pay enough attention to you, just come to me." White grinned engagingly, "I dance a mean foxtrot."

"Thank you, Mr. White, but I think I'll stay with him for the evening. And let me introduce you."

Gus made short work of greeting the men around him, then ushered Caroline to the dance floor for a waltz. She moved smoothly, following his lead with a grace that was second nature. "You do look beautiful, you know."

"Thank you," she smiled up at him, her eyes bright with excitement.

"You're welcome. There's just one thing wrong."

Her smile didn't dim. In fact, her eyes narrowed and

she tilted her head in suspicion. "Okay, I'm not wearing jeans coated with sawdust or clothes soaked through with river water. But it wasn't on the suggested dress list—"

"I guess the dress will do. But the thing is—" He chuckled and shifted her away from an older couple who were more enthusiastic than talented in their dance moves, and headed toward the edge of the room. "I just wanted to bring your attention to the small faux pas you made in your wardrobe. Your hair—"

"Yes?"

He loved the way she drawled the word, along with the tilt of her mouth as she tried to avoid smiling.

"It should be down, not in that twirly style." He released his grip on her hand to wave his hand near her ear.

Her hand came up and caught his in the next instant. "Oh no, you don't. It took me too long to get it this way. So, what's wrong with it?"

"Nothing, the light just doesn't catch it like it does when it's down around your shoulders." He squeezed her hand and ended the dance with a turn.

She didn't reply but glanced around the room. He offered her his arm and guided her to the refreshment table. "Nothing to say?"

She glanced up at him with a smile that threatened his breath control. "I'm planning my revenge. Travis will be pleased to know that you own a powder blue tux."

"Honey, he has one in yellow. It was his wedding."

When her laughter rang through the room she'd made his night.

Caro sighed as she eased her feet from her heels. "That was fun, but I'm glad it's only once a year."

Gus grinned at her then return his gaze to the road. "You don't want to do it again?"

"Sure, it's a great opportunity." She eyed him, then added, "All of the papers in the South want to cover this event. To be chosen as a correspondent is a big thing."

"So it's just the job."

"And the chance to be Cinderella for a night." She laughed and arched her feet. "But I bet Cindy never had aching feet like mine."

"In those glass shoes? Nah, next best thing to Dr. Scholl's, I'm sure," he quipped back. Caro shifted her position so that her back rested against the door of the car. Gus still wore his jacket, thanks to the spring chill in the air, but he'd gotten rid of the tie and loosened his shirt at the neck. He drove the car with confidence, maneuvering through the interstate traffic with a sure hand.

"You were good at getting the information you needed. I bet few of the guests there realized you were interviewing them." Gus's tone had an edge to it that made Caro wonder.

"It's my job. I don't impose myself on anyone. I don't quote out of context and I don't do character assassination."

"You're one of the few that have those standards, though."

Caro sat up at that. "I don't think so. What have you got against newspaper reporters, anyway?"

"Just that a lot of them don't care what they have to do to get a story. Or who they have to hurt." His tone had gone from an edge to grating and sharp.

"Well, not me. I have to sleep at night and things like that don't fit my sleep factor. And a lot of my friends are the same. Don't paint us with the same brush, Gus. It's not fair."

"Honey, if I'd lumped you into the same category with the bottom feeders I've had contact with, we wouldn't have been dating."

She sat in silence as he drove, then steered the conversation back to common interests. By the time they'd pulled into her parking lot, the tension had lessened and she felt more comfortable.

She slid her feet into the shoes reluctantly, then allowed Gus to help her from the car. They walked in silence to her door, where she turned to him. "Thanks for coming with me tonight. You made it easier for me to do my job."

He stood and looked at her, his warm topaz gaze flowing over her like a warm river. "I can't say I enjoyed it, at least the crowd and all." He smiled then, "But I did like watching you shine." He lifted a hand and smoothed her upswept hair at her ear. "You sparkle like the moon in summertime."

Her skin tingled from his touch and Caro held her breath as his hand drifted to the nape of her neck. With a gentle tug he pulled her toward him and she tilted her face to meet his lips. Warmth spread from her lips to her toes as they kissed and she grasped the lapels of his jacket to steady herself. Finally, eons later he shifted away from her. "I'll see you in the morning."

"What are we doing then?" She whispered.

"Don't know. But we'll do it together." He wheeled around and strode down the hall. Caro sighed as she let herself into her apartment. Gus might not like reporters, but he did like her. And it was enough.

Chapter Ten

"What the hell is this?" The city desk editor glared at Caro, his face covered in red splotches. He clutched the latest *Single Life* column in his fist and waved it in front of him.

"My column for the week," Caro came farther into the room and sat in the chair opposite Mr. Wheaton and waited. In the week since the Gala she'd been out with Gus every day, meeting him for breakfast at a small family owned eatery, renting movies in the evening and cuddling on the couch at her apartment, taking simple walks and drives in the country and talking. The argument they'd had over reporters' morals drifted away and she'd fallen deeper under his spell.

The night before, she'd given into the temptation

and written her column, expounding on finding the right guy. She hadn't admitted it to Gus, but once he read the article, he'd know her feelings. Maybe she needed to talk to him *before* the column came out.

"You can't print this crap. Do it over."

"Mr. Wheaton, I don't have time to write another column, it's going to print in an hour."

If it was possible, his face grew more flushed and even appeared to expand, like a frog before it croaked. She stifled a giggle at the image.

He prized the twisted paper loose and flattened it on the desk. With a biting tone, he read, " 'Meeting a nice guy is difficult in this day and age but when you do meet him, it's hard to let go. My guy is one of the best. He's a simple guy, works hard in his job and really doesn't care for the trappings of the 'get it all world.' " Good Lord, Paul, don't you have any pride?"

"I'm sorry, sir?"

Wheaton threw the article down, the disgust evident on his face. "The articles you've written for the *Single Life* haven't had the zing they had when Stone and Morgan wrote them, but I let you get away with them 'cause the readers still liked them. Found them refreshing and all that bunk. But now, this is more like one of those cheesy advice columns. Ratings are going to tank."

"I don't agree. Most of the letters and e-mails I've

read indicate the public like following romances, either online, on television, or in print. My column is just the next step in the chain, my chain."

"Well, don't be surprised when you get choked on that chain." Wheaton leaned forward and continued, "If this column tanks because of you, you're off of the paper."

Caro kept her gaze on his, determined not to blink first. She'd only told the truth, as always, and it would come out in the end. It had to.

She left the newspaper on time, her mind awash with the possibilities. If the *Single Life* flopped in Atlanta while doing well in the other cities, her life as a reporter would be over. Her friendship with Laney would survive, it had survived more disasters than this.

If, on the other hand, the column was accepted by the public, she could continue with both columns and life would go on as before. With one variable she couldn't control. Gus. What would be his reaction when he read the column?

"As if I'm going to wait for that," she muttered and reached into her purse for her cell phone, then quickly returned both hands to the steering wheel. Her car, the trusty hand-me-down from her father on her college graduation, suddenly started making noises she didn't recognize. Sputters, followed by odd clicks kept her on edge for miles, afraid she'd

The Single File

stall in the heavy traffic and cause more trouble for herself and the other drivers. She decided to detour to Gus's garage and found an exit onto the country road.

She cautiously reached for the phone again and dialed the garage number. When Travis answered, she described the sounds and sighed in relief when he urged her to come on in.

"Do you think it'll be something simple?" Translate, cheap to repair.

"Gus and I'll find the problem, don't worry. Bring her on in."

She ended the call and drove. "Come on, girl, don't give up on me, now." She patted the steering wheel as the car's sputter smoothed out a bit.

By the time she got to the garage, Gus's truck was parked beside the gas pumps. He strode toward her as she pulled the car in front of the gaping bay. He opened the car door for her to exit and hugged her.

"What's up, sweetheart? Travis said you're having some trouble with the Volvo."

"She's sputtering and making some weird clicking sounds. I know she's old and clunky, but she's mine." She felt close to tears and very foolish but his look of understanding made it less troublesome.

"We'll take care of her, okay? Listen, you can drive my truck home and I'll call you later."

"I want to stay."

He nodded and tucked her into his side, leading her to the bay. "Okay, we'll order some pizza and take a look."

She sat, paced, and stood over him and Travis as they muttered about converters and fuel lines. Finally, two long hours later, Gus walked to the work bench and wiped his hands with a rag. "Honey, you need a new fuel injector."

She heaved a breath she hadn't realized she was holding then asked, "How much?"

"I don't know yet. We'll have to order the part from the dealership, if they have it for this model." He opened the pizza box and surveyed its contents then turned away.

Travis wheeled up with a cordless phone. "I checked and they'll get the part to us by the end of the week."

Caro glanced at both men. "Will the car hold up til then?"

"It should. But I'd feel better if you took another car."

"Gus, I can't drive a stick shift and besides, I'd look silly in that truck."

"But what about the Crown Vic?"

She shuddered, "No way. I'd ding it within an hour of driving it. No, if you think the Volvo will be okay til the part comes in, I'll stick with her. She's been good to me."

"Fine. But keep your cell on so you can call me if you have a problem."

She grinned up at his stern expression, "Yes sir."

As she approached the car her stomach sent out a loud growl. She flushed at the low laughter behind her and turned to send a mock frown at Travis and Gus. "I wouldn't be hungry if you two hadn't hogged the pizza."

Gus chuckled. "Want me to make up for it and take you out to dinner?"

"We both smell like oil and other garage stuff. I'd rather have something at home." And that'd give her the opportunity to talk to him about the *Single Life* column.

"Okay, my house or yours?"

"My apartment is closer. I'll run by and pick up some stuff and meet you there at around seven?"

"Deal. It'll give me time to wash off all the 'garage stuff'," he finished with a grin and a kiss.

She stopped at the grocery on her way home, since all she had in her fridge at the moment was a jar of green olives and coffee creamer. She stewed for too long over roasted chicken, frozen lasagna and desserts before deciding on the real man food. Finally, stocked with baking potatoes, thick rib eyes and salad, she stopped off at the dessert aisle and grabbed a cheesecake.

After cursing the greater Atlanta traffic, she finally made it home by six. She quickly scrubbed and foil wrapped the potatoes and put them in the oven before stowing the rest of the items in the refrigerator.

A shower, fast hair dry and makeup job and she was ready. She turned on the news for background noise and set out the steaks for broiling then tossed the salad and set the small table in the dining area. All the while she practiced her speech.

A few minutes after seven, the doorbell sounded. Caro checked the neck of her mint green sweater and smoothed her dark brown slacks before answering. Gus stepped in, a bouquet of flowers in one hand, much like the ones he'd brought when they first started dating, and a paper bag in the other.

She extended her hand to accept the flowers only to have him withdraw his hand. "Only for a price," he teased.

Her head tilted and her hand still outstretched, she smiled. "What's the price?"

He placed the bag on a side table and enveloped her hand in his larger one then drew her to him. "A kiss."

"Okay—"

"For each flower."

Caro giggled, her tension easing as minutes passed. "How many did you get?" She eyed the multicolored array of flowers, lilies, tulips, and smaller unidentifiable blossoms.

"At least two dozen," he grinned. "I counted them, but I'm sure I missed some of the little ones."

She gave in and laughed then stood on tiptoe to give him a quick smack on the lips then wrapped her hand around the blossoms. "That one's on account."

He turned over the bouquet at her slight tug. "On account of what?"

"On account of I have two steaks ready for you to grill."

Gus retrieved the bag and followed her.

She glanced at the plain brown wrapper, "What's in the bag?"

"I noticed you like ice cream so I stopped at Baskin Robbins and picked up some."

She grinned, he was getting to know her. She led the way into her small kitchen and unwrapped the foil covered platter to reveal the rib eyes. He leaned in close over her shoulder and gazed into the chilled container.

"Honey, you've got me pegged." He rolled up his shirt sleeves then flexed and extended his arms. "Watch and learn."

He washed his hands and removed the steaks. A few shakes of the salt and pepper shakers and he was ready. Caro stood by as he opened the oven door, removed the hot potatoes and placed the steaks on a baking dish.

After he'd adjusted the oven temperature, he

turned and washed his hands again. Caro arched an eyebrow at him and handed him a paper towel. "That's it? The whole he-man grill thing? Salt and pepper?"

"It's not the ingredients, sugar. It's the method that makes it tasty."

She shook her head and rummaged through the cabinet for a baking dish and cover. She popped the baked potatoes inside and covered them then set them on the rear vent burner to stay warm. When she turned she met his gaze. "Something to drink?"

"Sure. The steaks shouldn't take long. Medium well?"

"Um–hmm."

Caro poured a couple glasses of tea and faced him as he leaned against the counter opposite the oven. A warm glow lit her from within, not the heat from the oven, but from his gaze.

"Can we leave the oven for a few minutes?"

"It should be okay. Let's go sit," he cupped the small of her back with his free hand and led her into the living room.

Caro sank onto the sofa and when he sat beside her, leaned into the steady strength of his side as he tucked her in close with his arm around her shoulders. Caro let her head drop onto his shoulder and breathed in the scent of him. Soap, cologne and underneath it all, Gus.

The Single File 155

He let her stay there for a few minutes. When he did speak, his voice rumbled into her ear, "You asleep?"

She nuzzled in closer, "Almost. Do you need to check on the steaks?"

"Yeah. Want a refill?"

She straightened, sighing. "No, I don't think I've taken more than one drink from it."

He disappeared around the corner and into the kitchen. She sipped her drink as the sounds of life drifted into the room. The oven door opening, the clang of metal against metal and the muffled sound of his footfalls as he returned to the living room.

"Steaks are almost there," he lowered himself back onto the sofa beside her. "Now, where were we?"

She tilted her head up for his kiss, content to her bones, yet a frissom of anxiety ran through her.

When the soft kiss ended she straightened and faced him, her side still in contact with his but with breathable distance. "I need to tell you something."

He arched a brow in question and she continued, "I wrote a few of the columns that are covering the Gala. The one appearing tomorrow concerns you."

Where his expression had been relaxed and open, now it tightened. She wondered at the change in his look but needed to go on. "I confessed to something."

"Go on." He didn't move from her, yet she felt his distance.

Caro's every instinct was to look away from him, to hide the emotion she was convinced lay in her face, but she met his gaze squarely. "I admitted to some feelings for you."

Gus sat, silently eyeing her. A moment passed, then another. Finally, when she was sure she'd scream from the pressure of his scrutiny, he rose and started from the room. "I need to check the steaks."

"You need to—" She rose and followed him. "Is that it?"

He opened the oven door, releasing warm appetizing aromas that any other time would have made her mouth water. Now she just wanted to shake him until he responded.

"I'm all but declaring that I love you on the town square. And you have to check the steaks?"

He used a dishtowel to remove the platter of meat and placed it on the top of the stove then flicked off the oven. At last he turned to her, the dishtowel in his hand.

"I needed time."

"Time? Time for what?" Time to think of a nice way to let her down? Time for her to prepare for the public humiliation?

"Time for me to do this." He advanced, clasped her face between his hands and leaned in. This kiss, unlike the sweet one in the living room, sent a message. Dimly, she thought she should think of what the message was, but found she'd rather just give in to the warmth of his touch, the pleasure of his kiss.

When they finally ran out of breath and had to part, he set her away from him enough to meet her eyes. "I love you, Caroline. Never doubt that."

She sighed and returned to his embrace, content to stay there and put off any future. Now was just fine, thanks.

The rest of the evening was a blur for Caro. The meal could have been gourmet quality or sawdust, she didn't care. From his actions, neither did Gus. They sat at the table, their food largely untouched, and talked. Talked of the times they'd spent together, of the future that lay ahead. And most of all, of the wonder of finding each other. Caro learned about Gus's college days, his one serious relationship and why he'd been so reticent with her on their first meeting. She had the feeling he still held things from her, but it'd come, she knew it.

At the end of the evening, Gus stood at the door. "I've got a few things to get done tomorrow, call you in the evening?"

Caro smiled her acceptance and enjoyed the lingering goodnight kiss. As she prepared to turn in, she wondered at her luck. Who would think a garage mechanic could turn out so great, and that she would meet him when she had least expected it?

* * *

Gus found it hard to turn his attention to the work of a company CEO the following day. His attention had been split today between contacting a contractor for the South Carolina property he'd finally gotten the contract for, solving disputes between two garages in Alabama and hiring another VP to take the load off of Dave. Now, the end finally in sight, he relaxed back in his chair and let his mind wander.

The evening before, he'd made a commitment to Caroline. Even if he hadn't asked her to marry him yet, he knew he would. And she would say yes, he was sure.

It was time, time to trust again. And Caroline was the one to trust, she'd proven it time and again. When he told her of his failed romance, she'd been righteously irritated. In turn he'd been surprised at her views on her looks, she didn't consider it a blessing that she was too beautiful for words.

One last contract to review, and he'd be finished at the office. With the life ahead of him with Caroline, the time he had with her seemed more precious than ever.

Dave stuck his head in the door, "Boss, have you seen the paper today?"

Gus glanced up from his reading. "No, didn't take the time this morning. Why?"

Dave advanced into the room, a folded newspaper

in his hand. "There are a couple of things that might interest you."

Gus grinned, his thoughts turning to Caroline's column. "Yeah I know."

Dave stopped, his hand outstretched to hand the paper over. "You knew about the business editor's opinion piece?"

"The business—Let me see." Gus took the paper and unfolded it. Lane had it opened to the business section, which made sense. The MBA usually read the business section before he read the headlines, more concerned about the market than war or famine.

Gus frowned at the sight of the byline on the business op ed piece. Franklin Jones. A bottom dweller, as far as Gus was concerned, Jones had almost destroyed a friend whose business went through a downturn. Only his strong personality and connections kept the business afloat and his family intact. That Jones had used bad information to print lies and fallacies about a legitimate businessman was bad enough, that he didn't retract anything until two years and a court order later sealed his reputation, as far as Gus was concerned.

"Jones' column. Give me the short version."

Dave sank into the visitor's chair and propped his bent elbows on his knees. "He mentions you, a reporter that works at the Globe and some social thing you went to."

"And?"

Dave, a wolf when it came to negotiating contracts, froze at Gus's request. He gestured toward the paper, "You need to read it, Gus."

The paper rustled as Gus lifted it and read. The farther he got into the article, the angrier he became.

It's amazing what business can be done at a social event, even the biggest social event of the Atlanta elite. The bankers and brokers meet quietly and decide our futures over canapés with both the powerful and not so influential. Even the beautiful society reporter wined and dined for her date, garage mini-magnate of the south. When a reporter presents herself as the innocent falling for a wholesome guy (see the *Single Life* current issue) it's interesting. That the same reporter was heard mentioning that her date was a rich guy ripe for the picking— Well, it's a superb spectator event, even for the most callous reporter.

Gus didn't bother finishing the rest of the tirade. Instead, he crumpled the paper in his hand, stood and stalked from the room. Behind him, Dave muttered something, but the crimson haze of anger muffled it.

He forced calm into his system before he unlocked the door to his truck. As he twisted the ignition, he wondered where to go, to get rid of the red-hot rage. The garage was out, Travis would be determined to talk it out, try to "reason" with him. Caroline? He had to get into shape before meeting her. So, he started toward the one place he knew he could work out the frustration.

Three hours later, he stopped and wiped the film of sweat from his forehead. The tree fallen by a late winter storm, had become a healthy pile of firewood. The house would have plenty of fuel for heat in the coming winter. More importantly, Gus felt in control, more able to think clearly.

He carried the ax as he walked, picking up the chain saw and discarded shirt from the ground as he headed for the house and a cool shower. There was a small buzz sounding from his shirt pocket, which he ignored. The phone had been ringing since he arrived home. Once he had his shower, he'd deal with whatever he had to, on his terms.

Caro ended the call on her cell phone with a frown. She'd never been unable to reach Gus by his cell phone before. But now, in the space of two hours, she'd received nothing but voice mail.

An unknown worry nagged at her stomach and had prompted the calls. But he wasn't at the garage, Travis had been pretty uncommunicative, and now the cell phone. She sighed and reverted to the one place her mother had urged her never to call. "A southern lady just doesn't call a man at home before you're married, honey. It looks too desperate."

She dialed the number on her cell and pulled her car off the main highway and into a drive through lane at a fast food restaurant. Again, a message. "Hi, Gus. I was just calling to—well, I guess to just talk to you. Um, I miss you, I love you and I'll talk to you later, okay?"

She pushed the end button and tossed the phone onto the passenger seat with a snort of disgust. "Just what you need. You tell the world you love the man and can't think of what to say when you leave him a message."

She decided to focus not on the silly worry. It was probably just her superstitions, she'd never told a man she loved him before, after all. So, she'd focus on her job, getting the interview with the mayor's wife on her favorite charity, and plan on seeing Gus that evening.

She unlocked her door with a sharp jerk and once the door was opened, dropped her purse and carryall onto the floor of her small foyer. "Lord, what a day."

Everything that could go wrong had done so. She'd let battery run down on her cell, her interview with the mayor's wife fell through, why she didn't know, and finally, her car, her trusty, old Volvo, had sputtered all the way home. Hopefully, the part for the car Travis and Gus said she needed would arrive before the old girl bit the dust.

She entered the living room area and glanced toward the kitchen counter and the phone answering machine. The little red light blinked frantically. Did she feel like checking them now? No, but Gus may have called—

She slipped off her heels on the way to the dividing counter and sat on the bar stool to retrieve the messages. There was a message from the office that her interview had been canceled, a call from her bank, a couple of hang-ups and Laney. "Hey, kiddo. Wanted to talk to you about this morning's column. Call me when you get in. I'll be in Tampa, so call me on my cell."

The column? Well, she hadn't told her best friend she planned to confess to whole city, so it made sense. She'd call after she had some food and talked to Gus, but not necessarily in that order.

She changed into comfortable knit pants and a T-shirt before pulling a meal from the freezer and popping it into the microwave. Then she plugged her cell phone into its charger, poured a glass of iced tea and sat at the counter to wait for her food.

She glanced at the phone. Should she call again or

wait for Gus? The battle between wanting to talk to him, make a connection, and a hard won sense of self resulted in her rising and retrieving her chicken marsala with rice dinner, and then walking into the living room to veg out for an hour.

She'd taken her first bite when the telephone rang. She all but sprinted to the base and plucked the cordless from its cradle. "Hello."

"Caroline, it's Gus."

She breathed a sigh. He sounded wonderful, stressed, but great. "Hi, I tried to call you earlier, your cell must have been off. Mine—"

"Sorry, I had a lot of stuff to get done. Listen, I need to discuss something with you. Can we meet somewhere?"

Her smile dimmed a little; boy, was he stressed. He never interrupted her, but then she didn't make a practice of rambling, either. "Sure, why don't you come over here, though? I don't have any food, but I can order out. Pizza, Chinese?"

"Whatever you want. I'll be over in about half an hour." He hung up before she could reply.

She dumped the frozen dinner down the disposal, called in an order for Chinese to deliver, and quickly changed her clothes. Gus had seen her in sloppier clothes than the sweats, but her training from childhood stuck. She'd meet her date with a neater outfit than workout clothes.

By the time Gus rang the doorbell she was ready. She smiled as she opened the door and leaned into him for a kiss. When it didn't come, she opened her eyes and peered at him.

"Anything wrong?"

He entered the foyer and closed the door behind him. "Let's sit." He cupped her elbow and with sure, firm pressure, led her to the living room.

Caro eyed him as she walked, unsure of his mood. He didn't seem upset, but intent and focused like she'd never seen him.

She sat on the sofa, ready for him to join her but he remained standing. He wore a suit, something she hadn't seen him in, other than the tuxedo he'd worn to the gala. But more than that, he wore an aura of authority she'd not experienced before. And while it might enhance his allure, it also made her uneasy.

"Have you read the paper today?"

"I beg your pardon?" What was this about?

"*The Globe,* have you read it?"

"No, I didn't get a chance, yet. Is it about my column? We talked about it last night—" she cut off at the slash of his hand.

"No, there was another column I found interesting."

Caro resisted the urge to rub her forehead. The situation grew more confusing by the minute, but for now, she'd play along. "I'll have to pick up a copy in the morning, when I get to work."

He reached in his coat pocket and retrieved a wrinkled, folded paper. "No need, I have it here." He opened the paper and handed it to her.

She shot a quick glance toward Gus then lowered her head and started to read. As she did, she was aware of him sitting in the easy chair, not the sofa beside her.

Horror, anger, and disbelief surged through her as she read the article. "I can't believe the paper printed this drivel."

"The *Globe* isn't a paper that prints unsubstantiated information, I've heard."

She arched an eyebrow and tossed the paper to the sofa beside her. "Don't throw that back at me, Gus."

"So, you didn't interview the president of First National?"

"You know I did, you were there the entire evening."

"But I was across the room most of the time, out of your way. Out of the way but not out of line of sight."

"Line of sight? You make the whole event sound like a sporting event." She held on to her temper with an effort.

"Your words, not mine."

"You're not making sense. I had a job to do that night, and I did it. If you hadn't wanted to go with me, you should have said so."

"I wanted to go with the woman I thought you were, the woman who hammered and ate hot dogs. Said you preferred them."

"I do, and you did."

"No, I didn't. I went with the woman mentioned in that damn article." He gestured toward the discarded paper.

"You believed that?" She stood and faced him, her face heating. "That—that trash? If you believe I play people just to get a story, that I'd lie to someone to get ahead—"

"That you'd pretend not to know who I am? I think I do believe that. And why shouldn't I? You're a reporter, experienced at ferreting out details and facts. The fact you thought I was a garage mechanic was too good to be true."

"You *are* a garage mechanic."

"I have twenty garages, spread across a five state radius. And you knew it."

"Twenty? What are you talking about?"

"Hill's Garage Works, my company. The 'mini-magnate,' I think Jones termed me. Or should I say, the 'rich guy ripe for the picking'."

"You're rich?" She realized she sounded like a dumb parrot but the whole thing was too much to absorb. Then it hit her. "You lied to me?"

"I didn't lie."

"You told me you were a garage mechanic, that you owned the garage with Travis."

"And I do," he started pacing, "My first garage, followed by the rest."

"And you lied." Just like all the rest.

"No, I didn't lie, I just didn't tell you anything unnecessary."

"Unnecessary? I told you I loved you and you thought it wasn't important to tell me?" She tried to control the volume of her voice, but couldn't resist the quiver of anger.

"Useless information, since you already knew. And used it to your advantage."

She pulled her anger in, used it to wrap around the chill inside. Maybe it could get her through this. "I did what you did, Gus. I protected myself. And I told you what you needed to know. Only what you needed to know."

He smiled, but it wasn't the warm, enticing smile she was used to. This grimace was cold, chilling. "So, that's that. Well, it's been fun."

He turned and walked toward the door. As he approached, the doorbell rang. Gus twisted the knob, there stood a delivery girl with bags of Chinese takeout. He pulled his wallet from his back pocket and extracted a bill. Thrusting it into the girl's hand, he took the bags and set them on the floor. Caro followed, her only intent to close the door and lock him outside so she could wallow. As he stepped through the doorway, he shot over his shoulder, "One last dinner on me."

Chapter Eleven

"Caro? Are you in there?" The knocking on the door became a pound and the reverberation of it thrummed through her aching brow. She shoved a pillow over her head and pressed it against her ear, trying to force out the sound.

"Caro! I'm coming in."

"Noo." She mumbled.

"Oh my God." Laney entered the bedroom and jerked the blanket off Caro. "You're pathetic. How many days have you been in here?"

"I don't know, two, three." Caro growled and reached for the blanket, which Laney tugged away.

"Get out of bed."

"Go away."

"I'm staying until you look human again."

Caro glared at her friend as she starting picking up cookie sleeves and ice cream containers. "Why did I give you a key?"

"Because you trust me. Now get up and take a shower."

"I don't want to." Caro winced at the sound of her own voice, whiny and self pitying.

"I don't care. Get up and go or I'll put you in there with your pajamas on." Laney turned and started out of the room, "I'm starting some coffee. It'll be ready when you're done."

Caro considered retrieving her blanket and going back to sleep but the sudden clatter of another person in the apartment kept her awake. She growled then sat up in bed. Her foot butted against an Oreo package, the rustle of the cellophane thundering in the room.

As she surveyed the room Caro became aware of the mess. Piled among the food containers were the usually pressed, folded and scented clothing, rumpled and, she was sure, stained with chocolate.

"God, I've turned into my mother." She moaned and headed toward the bathroom. Her mother's history of taking to her bedroom when she argued with Caro's father had influenced her daughter to become the opposite, neat to a fault and determined to be independent. Now, Gus Hill had managed to deal her a debilitating blow with his allegations.

"But no more pity party, girl." She stripped down and turned on the shower then stepped in and stood under the water flow, letting its warmth seep into her chilled body.

By the time she climbed out of the shower, dressed and dried her hair, the most obvious of the food containers and trash had been cleared from the bedroom and the smell of coffee permeated the room.

She padded into the kitchen and found Laney bent over the refrigerator, peering inside. "You probably won't find much." Caro sat on one of the bar chairs at the counter, inexplicably exhausted, though she'd stayed in bed for days.

"I brought some milk and bread." Laney stood with a tub of margarine and an almost empty jar of jam in her hands. She nudged the fridge door closed with her hip and strode to the counter. In a few sure movements she popped a couple of slices of bread in the toaster and poured coffee for both of them.

Caro accepted the coffee gratefully and sipped the black brew. She propped her hand on her chin and watched as Laney spread margarine and jam on the toasted bread then deliver it to Caro on a napkin. "Your dishes are in the dishwasher, so this'll have to do."

"I'm not hungry."

"When did you eat last?" Laney sipped her own coffee.

Caro shrugged, "I don't remember."

"If the state of the dishes are any indication, it's been too long." Laney nodded toward the toast, "Eat. And I'm not going to ask what you ate last, I've seen the evidence."

Caro picked up the bread to stop the nagging and nibbled on the edge. She chewed on the multigrain toast then forced herself to swallow. "Why are you here?"

"Why do you think? We've been trying to call you for four days. I even tried calling from the airport when my plane got in. When your answering machine and voice mail started kicking back at me I decided I needed to see if you were still alive."

"I called and told you not to worry—"

"Four days ago, Caro." Laney leaned over the counter, her face inches away from Caro's. "I was worried."

"Sorry." Caro replied flatly. "I needed to be alone for awhile, to think."

"Well, you've had plenty. It's time to rejoin the human race."

"Rat race, you mean." Caro shoved the plate of bread away, the single bite barely visible. Laney didn't argue with her, but stared through narrowed eyes. A minute passed then she straightened and carried the plate to the sink.

Caro stared at the countertop, wondering where

she'd build up the energy to do as Laney said, go back to work, go to the grocery, do her laundry.

Laney turned from her task and leaned against the sink, "So, you're going to let him get away with it."

Caro stirred herself out of her stupor, "Let who get away with what?"

"Franklin. He's been strutting around the office like a rooster, bragging about how he brought you down."

"He's what?"

"You heard me. The jerk is saying you've quit, you're not coming back to the paper. That you're too embarrassed."

Caro felt her eyes dry out from staring but she couldn't look away. The lethargy that had overtaken her in the past days vanished in that instant, replaced with cleansing, rejuvenating anger.

"What time is it?" She searched the room for her wall clock, blocked by Laney.

"Around eleven, why?"

"I'm going in to the paper." Caro stood and headed toward her bedroom.

"That's my girl," Laney shouted behind her.

An hour and a half later, armed with a designer dress, makeup and her favorite shoes, Caro strode into the newsroom. The usual buzz died as she advanced, replaced by silence interspersed with the occasional whisper or hiss of a lowered voice.

She ignored everyone, intent on getting to the lifestyle editor's office. Julia, as always, had her music on full volume. Caro hammered on the door then opened it to the din of electric guitar and a bass beat. Julia was bent over her desk, intent on proofing copy. Maybe the unusual breath of fresh air roused her, but she lifted her head and took in Caro. She straightened and, reaching behind her, flicked off the boom box.

"Do I still have my job?"

"Your job? Yeah, we ran one of the columns you wrote on the gala. Good thing you'd turned in several at once." A frown passed her editor's face before she continued, "Why?"

Caro shook her head then turned to exit.

"Are you feeling better?" Julia's question wheeled her back around.

"Sorry?"

"Morgan said you had the flu or something. So are you feeling better? Ready to come back?"

"I'm fine, thanks." Caro hadn't made it to the door when another question stopped her.

"When are you going to go after Franklin?"

"In about three minutes." If he was in the office, he was in her sights.

"Good, I'll be there." Julia grinned and popped a piece of gum.

Caro grimaced as she shut the office door behind

her. That was all she needed, an audience. And she still had to figure out what she would say when she confronted Franklin.

She dropped her briefcase and purse off at her desk the surveyed the newsroom. He wasn't in the open room so, if he was in the building at all, it was in his office.

She straightened her shoulders and headed down the aisle. The anger she'd fostered while getting ready evaporated with each step, the adrenaline rush long gone.

The office door to the business editor's work area was closed. But, unlike Julia English who kept her door closed out of respect of her coworker's ears, Franklin Jones' door was meant to separate him from what he considered to be subordinates.

She didn't knock, he wouldn't admit her anyway. Before she opened the door, she took a deep bracing breath. "Jones, I need a word."

Franklin hid the *Money* magazine beneath his blotter and stood. "Caroline, you're here?"

"Where did you think I'd be, Franklin? Cowering at home?"

He quickly recovered his surprise and replaced it with a sneer. "Haven't you been doing just that?"

"A momentary weakness. And it gave me time to think, Franklin."

"Think of what? How you made a fool of yourself in not one, but two columns?"

"No, of why you'd want to lie about me," she blocked the doorway, not entering but not letting him exit either. "I didn't think you were so insecure about your job, Franklin, that you'd try to demean another reporter to solidify your position."

Behind her the whispers grew close and she became aware of a mill of people behind her. So, the whole office wanted to hear? Fine. She'd made her life public and she'd accept the consequences.

"I don't have to do anything to keep my job, unlike you." He spit the words at her.

"Don't you? Oh, I'm sorry, I thought it was professional jealousy that drove you to slander. I guess I was mistaken, it was personal. That makes it better." She finished with a heavy dose of sarcasm.

His flush blotched his thin face and crept up into his thinning hair line. "I don't have to take this."

Julia stuck her head into the doorway, just beside Caro. "Oh, I think you do, Frankie. Go ahead, Caroline."

"I didn't use my relationship with Gus Hill to influence anyone, to get any interviews. And that drivel you had printed? It's evidence, Franklin. In a case of libel and slander, it'll be a great tool for me to use."

The red stain on his face faded in an instant, replaced by chalk white. Franklin slumped into his chair. "I just wanted you to notice me."

"No, you wanted me to be more than a coworker. And when I didn't agree to date you more than the couple of times we went out, you decided to get back at me." Caro glared at him. "Well, pat yourself on the back, Jones. Thanks to you, I'll have to rebuild my influence with the social elite in this town. But at least I haven't breached the scope of *my* job. I doubt that the managing editor appreciates your personal slants in the business column."

She strode out of the office and to her desk, her head held high. By the time she sank into her chair, her knees were wobbling, but she kept her expression calm. She flicked on the computer and waited for it to boot up and flipped through her date book, pretending to look for appointments.

Laney approached her, her expression intent. "You okay?" she whispered as she handed Caro a sheath of blank paper.

"Yeah. Give me something to do, quick." *Before I throw up.*

"Okay. Let's go out and do some field work." Laney shot her a grin. "At the mall."

Caro managed a weak grin, then shook her head. "I've got to get my car fixed, I can't afford to go shopping for a while."

"Okay, what did you have on tap for the next *Single Life* column?"

My engagement. "A profile of the matchmaker I met."

"I thought you'd already done the article on matchmaking."

"I did, but I wanted to go more in depth. I wanted to highlight her dual roles in both my society column and the *Single Life* column, matchmaking and dress design."

"Huh?" Laney's confusion lightened Caro's mood a bit.

"Miriah designed the dress I wore to the gala. She's doing the matchmaking as a favor to her aunt. So, I wanted to tie in my society column and the *Single Life* column, do a human interest story."

"Okay, let's go talk to her."

Caro shook her head. "You don't have to go with me. I'll be fine. And I'll get the interview done faster if you don't go." She retrieved her purse and briefcase and turned the computer monitor off.

"You need to check your e-mail, you know." Laney followed her as she made her way to the exit.

"I know, but it'll wait til tomorrow." When she had a fresh infusion of courage, she'd tackle the fallout from Franklin's column.

When she started her car, it sputtered, reminding her of the task she had ahead of her. She'd have to find another garage to order the part and have it installed. Maybe she should do that first, before the interview. With her luck lately, she'd be stranded on the interstate if she didn't take care of it now.

She headed back into the newspaper office, intent on calling garages for estimates. Laney glanced up from her desk, "What'd you forget?"

"Nothing. The sputter in my car's getting worse. I decided to do that first, then worry about the interview."

"Are you going into Gus's garage?"

"No. I'm calling another place."

"But—"

"No, Laney."

"Caro, did you think that they'll have to eat the cost of the part if you don't pick it up?"

"They can send it back."

"Not necessarily. You need to call and see."

"Laney, I've already faced down one person today, I don't think I can do another one."

"You don't have to just, call and find out about the part. I'll go over and pick it up for you, if I have to."

"Fine." She picked up the phone and before she could think better of it, dialed the garage.

Travis answered with his usual cheerful tone.

"Hi, Travis, it's Caroline. I just wanted—"

"Caroline! I've been leaving messages for you for days. Are you okay?"

"I'm fine. I just wanted to check on the fuel injector that you'd ordered. Has it come in?"

"Yeah, I've got it."

"Can you send it back?"

"Have you got somebody else to work on your car?"

"No, but—"

"Then bring it on in. We'll get to it this afternoon, get it back to you by tomorrow."

"I don't think—"

"Look, Caroline. You need your car worked on and if you order the part from someone else, it'll take another week at the least to get the repairs done."

"What if I come by and pick up the part then take it to someone else? Can I do that?" She knew she sounded desperate, but she couldn't deal with the possibility of seeing Gus again, not now.

After a long silence, Travis agreed. "Fine, come by around five. I'll have it ready for you to pick up."

Caro ended the call. There was another casualty of Franklin's column. Her budding friendship with Travis appeared to be over before it really began, yet she felt a twinge of regret.

She relayed the information to Laney, who sent her a sympathetic look. "Need me to go with you?"

"No. Just have the ice cream ready, just in case."

* * *

Caro spent the rest of the work day checking her emails and voice mail, then making response calls. She spent an hour erasing emails and messages, not bothering to count the number of times Laney and Travis had called, but gratified both cared so much. A pleasant surprise came from the work, though. Most of the calls were from readers, expressing their ire at Franklin's audacity and offering words of encouragement. The complaint calls and emails turned out to be the regular amount she always got.

At four-thirty, she tidied her desk and again exited the building, this time with the mass of people ending their day. She started the car and prayed her way to the garage. By the time she made it there, her nerves were frayed from worry that the car would stall and anxiety that she'd see something that reminded her of Gus. "As if I need that, everything I do reminds me of him, now."

She scanned the parking area for his truck. Not there. She quickly parked and shut off her ignition, wincing as the car sputtered even as the engine died. A few feet away, the open bay doors yawned like a cave. From the depths of it country music flowed.

She entered the bay and glanced around. Travis was no where in sight. "Travis?"

"Be there in a sec." From the direction of his voice, he was in the rear supply room.

She walked to the work bench that was his usual station and waited, her pulse keeping time with the song that belted from the radio.

"Hey." He wheeled up to her.

"Hi. Do you have the part?"

"Yeah, I'll get it in a few minutes. I wanted to ask you something first." His eyes were steady on her and curious.

"Is it about the car?"

"No."

"Then it's not any of your business, Travis."

"Maybe it's not his, but it is mine." The deep tone sounded behind her.

Oh God. She didn't turn around, she couldn't.

"Caroline," Gus's hands cupped her shoulders and turned her with a gentle but firm movement. "Will you answer one question?"

"One?" She whispered.

"Only one. The only one I need to know."

She nodded, her eyes scanning his face. He looked tired, as tired as she felt after days of pining for him.

"Do you love me?"

The one question that opened her soul up to him, made her vulnerable. "Yes."

His intent stare melted as he smiled. "I love you."

"I didn't know who you were, Gus. I didn't use you to do anything."

"I know. I knew it all along, but I let my pride and past history mess with my head." His hands smoothed down her shoulders and cupped her upper arms.

His face blurred as tears filled her eyes. "Why didn't you tell me about your other garages? Didn't you trust me?"

"I'm sorry. I didn't tell you at first because I thought you were—"

"A gold digger?"

He shrugged. "Yeah, I'm sorry, but I did. My history with women who dress like you, look like you had been pretty bad, so I jumped to a conclusion before I got to know you." At her frown, he hurried to reassure her. "Then, as I got to know you better, went out with you, I realized you weren't like that, you're you. Beautiful, classy as hell, but real. By then, it just didn't matter."

She shook her head. "But that's a part of who you are, just like my job is part of me."

"Not as much as this place is a part of me. Maybe I didn't think about it because I didn't want to tempt you, I don't know. But I regret it. If I could do it again, I'd tell you."

She nodded and leaned into him, her head against his shoulder, and sighed. His arms came around her to enfold her. They stood there a few minutes then he continued, "You didn't give me much of a chance either, you know."

"I know. My past influenced me too. I've had a lot of guys lie to me and when I found out you'd not told me about your business, I just freaked."

His murmur of apology soothed her more than any speech could ever do and she relaxed into his embrace.

How long they stood there she didn't know, but a chuckle behind them brought her head up from its resting place against Gus's shoulder.

Travis sat in his chair, a box in his lap and the Bassets at his side, panting and tails wagging. "I guess we won't be working on the car tonight?"

"No. Not tonight. Tomorrow, we'll get to it." Gus set Caro away from him only to drape his arm around her waist and pull her to his side. "Tonight, I take Caroline out and celebrate."

"Celebrate what?" She smiled up at him.

"Our engagement?" He tilted his head at her.

Her smile widened and she nodded happily.

When she got home from the romantic dinner that night, she called Laney. When her friend answered the phone she squealed into the receiver, "I'm engaged!"

"You're kidding!"

"Nope. We're going shopping for the ring tomorrow, after he fixes my car."

Laney laughed, "Priorities?"

"Yep."

"Congrats, kid. Now, congratulate me." Laney purred over the phone.

"For what?"

"My engagement."

Caro jumped up and down. "Did you get engaged tonight too?"

"No, two days ago, in Tampa. I just didn't want to tell you."

"What about the *Single Life?*"

"We'll work it out. Maybe have different women and men go through the process and shadow them. After all, we won't be eligible."

Caro grinned, she couldn't stop grinning these days. "Well, so far, it's worked two for two. Maybe we can use that as a calling card. And I think I have the first candidate to shadow."